FIGHT TO THE DEATH

Still on his back, Pike could see the hatred in Iron Shield's eyes. The warrior had lost two of his braves and he aimed to have the white man's scalp. It was now or never.

Heaving with all his weight, Pike leaped off the ground and ran at the mounted Indian. He caught the man around the waist and pulled him from his horse in one mighty motion. Iron Shield was stunned at first, but soon regained his stance and fought hard. The two men rolled across the hardpacked clearing.

Using his strength and weight, Pike pinned the savage down against a flat rock, then pulled his bowie and thrust it into the Blackfoot warrior's gut. Iron Shield's eyes went wide, filled with anger and surprise, then suddenly went blank.

Pike stood up, staring at the dead Indian for a moment before wiping his knife on his buckskins and heading for the pony grazing nearby.

SCALE TO THE HEIGHTS OF ADVENTURE WITH

MOUNTAIN JACK PIKE

By JOSEPH MEEK

#1: MOUNTAIN JACK PIKE	(092-8, $2.95/$3.95)
#2: ROCKY MOUNTAIN KILL	(183-5, $2.95/$3.95)
#4: CROW BAIT	(282-3, $2.95/$3.95)
#5: GREEN RIVER HUNT	(341-2, $2.95/$3.95)
#6: ST. LOUIS FIRE	(380-3, $2.95/$3.95)
#7: THE RUSSIAN BEAR	(467-2, $3.50/$4.50)
#8: HARD FOR JUSTICE	(502-4, $3.50/$4.50)
#9: BIG GUN BUSHWACKER	(530-X, $3.50/$4.50)

Available wherever paperbacks are sold, or order direct from the Publisher. Send cover price plus 50¢ per copy for mailing and handling to Pinnacle Books, Dept. 657, 475 Park Avenue South, New York, N.Y. 10016. Residents of New York and Tennessee must include sales tax. DO NOT SEND CASH. For a free Zebra/ Pinnacle catalog please write to the above address.

MOUNTAIN JACK PIKE

#11 DEEP CANYON KILL

JOSEPH MEEK

PINNACLE BOOKS
WINDSOR PUBLISHING CORP.

PINNACLE BOOKS

are published by

Windsor Publishing Corp.
475 Park Avenue South
New York, NY 10016

Copyright © 1992 by Joseph Meek

All rights reserved. No part of this book may be reproduced in any form or by any means without the prior written consent of the Publisher, excepting brief quotes used in reviews.

Pinnacle and the P logo are trademarks of Windsor Publishing Corp.

If you purchased this book without a cover you should be aware that this book is stolen property. It was reported as "unsold and destroyed" to the Publisher and neither the Author nor the Publisher has received any payment for this "stripped book."

First Printing: November, 1992

Printed in the United States of America

PROLOGUE

The man in black had spent most of his life depending on the Lord to provide . . . and why not? He was, after all, a priest. Of late, however, he had found himself in situations where he'd had to provide not only for himself but for others as well.

Since traveling from the safety of the East to the mountains of the West, Father Adrian Smets had learned the true meaning of the saying "God helps those who help themselves."

He sat in front of his tent and looked over at the others, who were hovering by the fire for warmth. Two priests significantly younger than himself, Fathers O'Neil and Santini, held their hands over the fire, trying to work the circulation back into them. Father O'Neil, just out of seminary school, was only twenty-two years old. Father Santini, while carrying four or five years of seniority over Father O'Neil, was still only twenty-seven. Father Smets had been a priest longer than that.

Several women were part of the missionary force as well. Three ladies of varying ages and shapes also sought the warmth of the fire.

Sister Mary was perhaps the most comfortable of the

group, clad as she was in her habit. Of the women, she was in the same situation as Father Smets. She was easily the oldest of the three. At fifty, she was also the one they constantly had to slow down for. Father Smets, himself older even than Sister Mary, often insisted they slow the pace for her, and then confessed to himself later on, in the privacy of his tent, that he was easing up as much for himself as for her.

The other two missionary women were not nuns, and Father Smets often caught the men he had hired as guides staring at them. Sally Kennedy was thirty years old, and had been doing missionary work since she was twenty. Prior to that she had worked as a whore, until she met Father Smets. Now, dressed plainly, wearing no makeup, she was still a handsome woman.

The third woman was Gloria O'Malley, whom they all called "Glory." She was twenty-two years old, and she was Sally's discovery. The older woman had found her in an orphanage at age twelve and had taken her in. Sally had told Father Smets that there was something special about Gloria, something ... holy. Father Smets wasn't sure he agreed, but over the years Glory had proven to be quite effective in missionary work. She was a slender, blond woman with wraithlike beauty. Men were drawn to her, but when they realized that she had absolutely no interest in them beyond saving their souls they lost interest. Those who did not, ended up being saved.

Father Smets had been worried ever since he had hired their guides that perhaps he had placed them all in danger by hiring these particular men. Still, beggars could not be choosers, and when they had reached St. Louis and began looking for guides, these were the men they had found.

The leader was called Dolan, a large, shambling sort of man in his forties. He wore a beard, a great, wild, bushlike thing that he rarely kept clean, but the word Father Smets had received was that the man knew the mountains, and he had done nothing to disprove that. Indeed, he had gotten them this far, but of late the man's hot eyes had more and more been falling on Glory and Sally, and Father Smets was sure that he had no intention of being saved.

The other two men were called Mallory and Nolan, and were of the same cut as Dolan, though younger. Father Smets thought that Dolan had some sort of control over the two men. It seemed as if they would do anything he told them to do, and did very little thinking for themselves—except that lately they, too, seemed to be taking great interest in the movements of Sally and Glory.

Sister Mary approached Father Smets and held out a cup of steaming coffee.

"Father, why not come and sit by the fire?" she asked, crouching down next to him.

"I'm fine here, Sister," he said. He was sitting on a small foldout chair, with a blanket around him. He reached one hand out of the blanket to take the coffee, and sipped the hot liquid gratefully.

"Father," Sister Mary said, her voice becoming lower and somewhat conspiratorial, "I'm worried."

"About what, Sister?"

"These men you hired as guides."

"What have they done to worry you?"

"The same thing that is worrying you," she said. "I see you watching them, and we both see them watching Sally and Glory."

"Perhaps," Father Smets said, "but there is no harm in watching, is there?"

"Not as long as that is all they do," she said, "but what if they should decide to do more? What would we do then?"

"I will not let any harm come to Glory and Sally," Father Smets assured Sister Mary. "Or any of you, for that matter, Sister. Trust me."

"I have always done so, Father," she said. "All my life I have trusted you, and I've trusted in God, only now..."

Father Smets reached out and touched Sister Mary's shoulder.

"There is no shame in being afraid, Sister."

"Oh father—" she started, but she stopped short when they both heard a shout.

"Get away from her!" The voice was Sally's, and it was raised in anger.

"Father—" Sister Mary said in alarm.

Father Smets stood up quickly, letting the blanket fall to the ground. He was almost six feet four, and age had done nothing to decrease his height. He stood as straight and tall as he had forty years earlier.

"Stay here, Sister," he said, and started for the fire, where the commotion seemed to be centered.

As he approached he saw Sally standing directly between Glory and one of the guides, Nolan. Fathers O'Neil and Santini were also standing, but neither seemed ready to offer the women any physical assistance.

Coming from the other direction were Dolan and Mallory. As usual, they had put their bedrolls down away from the missionaries. Now they approached, wanting to know what was taking place, and ready to back up their friend.

"What's goin' on?" Dolan asked, beating Father Smets to the fire by a split second.

"Nothin'," Nolan said, glaring at Sally. "I was just tryin' to be friendly to the little lady, and this one jumps in my face."

"Mr. Dolan," Father Smets said, "I thought it was

understood that your men would stay away from the ladies."

Both Mallory and Nolan turned their eyes on Dolan to see what his response would be.

"Well now, Father," Dolan said, his tone almost apologetic, "that was then and this is now."

"Meaning what?"

"Meaning my men and I have decided to change the rules a little," Dolan said. "I mean, we ain't so bad, are we? Well, are we?"

"That's beside the point," Father Smets said.

"No, it ain't at all," Dolan said. "Come on, Father, you and these other fellas ain't usin' the women. Why can't we? We ain't gonna hurt them."

"The first one of you bastards tries to use me won't be usin' a woman for a long time," Sally said.

"She's got fire," Mallory said, licking his lips and staring at Sally again. "I been sayin' all along she's got fire, ain't I?"

"Yeah, you have, Mal. You ain't been a missionary all your life, have you, Missy?" Dolan asked, eyeing Sally.

"I've been around," Sally said.

"And what about your friend?" Dolan asked. "She been around, too?"

"You stay away from her."

"I think we've had about enough of this," Father Smets said. He walked over and stood next to Sally.

"Priest," Dolan said, "you ain't payin' us enough to travel with these women and pretend they ain't women."

"Enough of that talk!" Father Smets said stridently.

"Who's gonna stop us?" Mallory wanted to know. "You, priest? Or them?" He pointed to the two younger priests, who shrank back from his finger.

"Not them," Nolan said. "They're scareder than the women."

"Then you," Dolan said, looking at Father Smets. "You're gonna stop us?"

"I will not allow you to harm these women," Father Smets said. "If that means I must stop you, then I will."

Nolan and Mallory found that funny. Dolan, on the other hand, studied Father Smets with interest. Although in his sixties, the older priest was still an imposing figure. He had a full head of white hair, and he was taller than any of the mountain men.

"We ain't gonna hurt them, old man," Nolan said, "we're gonna pleasure 'em."

"I'd find more pleasure rutting with a goat," Sally said.

"That ain't nice talk, lady," Mallory said. "Which one you want, Nolan?"

Nolan licked his lips. "I want the young one."

"Fine," Mallory said, "the other one's got experience. I like a woman who knows what she's doin'."

Mallory and Nolan both looked at Dolan, and the other man nodded.

Nolan moved first, trying to get past Father Smets to reach Glory. The whole time the younger woman had been standing in fear, unable to move. Now she started, but was still unable to move away.

Father Smets put his hand flat against Nolan's chest and pushed the man back. Nolan was surprised at the old priest's strength and staggered back into Mallory, who steadied him.

"Come on, Nolan," Mallory said, "you gonna let some old man stop you?"

"You try it," Nolan challenged.

"Get out of my way, priest," Mallory said, reaching for him.

Father Smets reached out and took hold of Mallory's right wrist. Mallory frowned and tried to pull free, but couldn't. Father Smets did nothing more than hold him still.

"What's the matter?" Nolan asked, smiling. "Can't you get your hand free?"

Mallory pulled harder, but was unable to free himself from Father Smets' grip.

"Let go!" he said.

"I will let go when you agree to stop this nonsense," Father Smets said.

"Priest," Mallory said, taking out his knife with his left hand, "let . . . me . . . go!"

"No!" Sister Mary suddenly shouted, running toward them. "Don't hurt him!"

Dolan turned his head, saw the nun running toward them, slid his Kentucky pistol from his belt, aimed, and fired at her in one movement.

"No!" Father Smets shouted.

He released his hold on Mallory's arm and rushed to the fallen nun, followed closely by Sally. Fathers O'Neil and Santini still did not move, and Glory was unable to. Her eyes were wide with shock.

When Father Smets reached Sister Mary he raised her head, but saw that it was no use trying to help her; she was dead.

"Damn you!" Father Smets shouted at Dolan. "Damn you to hell!"

Dolan seemed taken aback by the outburst, as if the priest actually could damn him to hell.

"Kill the men," he said finally, "and then we'll have the women."

"No!" Father Smets said, standing and facing him. "No you won't."

"Get your rifles," Dolan said, "and kill the old priest first."

"Now you're talkin'," Nolan said. He turned to go for his rifle, but as he did an arrow appeared suddenly in his chest. He gagged and reached for the wooden shaft, turned toward Dolan, and then went to his knees. When he fell onto his face the arrow, instead of breaking, went completely through him, exiting out his back.

Glory, who had been unable to speak or move up to this point, screamed.

ONE

Jack Pike's favorite part of the Rockies were the highest peaks. Up there he could be alone with the snow, and the clouds, and whatever else he happened to believe in at the time. He needed to go up there every so often, especially when his outlook on life worsened. When that happened, he knew that he was not fit company for man or beast—not even for his friend Skins McConnell.

By the time Pike came down from the peaks he hadn't seen Skins McConnell for three months. They had agreed to meet in the Green River region not on any particular day, but during a particular week—this, the second week in March.

Pike felt calm, at peace with himself for the first time in a long time. During the course of the past year and a half, he had killed a lot of men—some unavoidably, some in rage. That fact ate at him for a long time, until he went up to the clouds. He had left the rage and the anger and the guilt up there, and he felt much better about it.

He knew where McConnell would probably be. They had camped near the Green River several times, and often used the same campsite. As he approached it he was surprised to see a tent. When he reached the camp he saw a couple of cold fires, and one fire burning. Around the fire were three figures who seemed to be huddling together for warmth. As they heard his horse they all turned. Their faces were white, and their eyes were wide with fear.

Pike rode up to the fire and stared down at the people. They were all young, two men and one woman. They all had blankets wrapped around them, and the woman had her head covered as well. Even when they saw who he was—he felt he was not projecting a menacing presence—the fear remained on their faces. Pike looked around but saw no one else. Surely these three babes in the woods couldn't be out here alone.

He saw signs that a struggle had occurred, and not too long ago. Now that he looked closer, he saw some arrows lying about, and off to one side he saw what looked like bodies covered by blankets.

"What happened here?" he asked.

The three people simply stared at him, as if struck dumb.

"I asked what happened here?" Pike repeated. When no one answered he asked, "Who's in charge here?"

He was waiting for one of the men to answer, but it was the young woman who finally lifted her arm, pointed at the tent, and said, "In there."

Pike turned in his saddle and looked at the tent, then dismounted.

"Take my horse," he said to the two men. He didn't care which one responded, but when neither did, he snapped, "Come on! One of you take my horse!"

Both men jumped to their feet, and it was then that Pike saw their collars and realized that they were priests. Both men reached for the reins in his hands, and he handed them to one of them.

"Thank you," he said. He guessed that maybe he

shouldn't have yelled at a priest—let alone *two*—but he decided not to apologize until he knew what he had walked into.

He turned and walked to the tent and entered without calling out.

"Hello," he said on entering.

There was a woman in the tent, and she was crouched down next to a man who was lying on a cot. The man was white-haired and old. He looked older still because he was injured, and the pain was plain in his face.

"What do you want?" the woman asked. Her posture was instantly defensive, but her attitude was far from that of the three people outside.

"What happened here?" Pike asked.

"Who are you?"

"If we keep asking questions," he said, "and no one answers any, we won't be able to help your friend."

Her attention turned to the man on the cot. "This is Father Smets."

"What happened to him?"

"We were attacked by Indians," she said. "Our guides were killed, and Father Smets was injured."

"Indians?" Pike said, frowning. "What kind?"

"I don't know what kind," the woman said, becoming annoyed. "Does that matter? They were savages and they attacked us."

"It's very unusual for Indians to harm a holy man, even a white one."

"No," she said, "you don't understand. The Indians didn't hurt him, our guides did."

"Your guides?"

"Look, I'll have to explain later," she said. "Can you help him? He's been shot."

"Is the ball still in there?" Pike asked.

"Yes," she said. "I can't—I don't know how to—I'm

not a nurse!"

"Do you have any control over those people outside?"

"Yes."

"Good," Pike said, moving closer to the man on the cot. He was very pale, and his lips were moving. Pike couldn't hear what he was saying, but it was a pretty safe bet that Father Smets was praying.

"Have them boil some water, and here . . . take this," he said, handing her his knife. "Have one of them hold it in the fire and then bring it to me."

"What are you going to do?"

"I'm going to get this ball out of his shoulder," Pike said. "After that, we can have a nice long talk."

She nodded, and left the tent with his knife.

After Pike successfully removed the ball from Father Smets' shoulder he bandaged the wound tightly. The old priest had passed out and Pike figured he'd be out for a while.

"Can we talk?" he asked Sally.

"I don't want to leave him alone."

"Get one of the others to stay with him."

She hesitated a moment, rubbing her arms. "All right. I'll be with you in a few minutes," she said.

"Have somebody put on a fresh pot of coffee, too," Pike said.

"We don't have any left."

"You can get it from my horse."

"All right."

Pike left her in the tent and went outside to look around. The other two priests were still huddled by the fire, and he could feel their fear in the air. Weren't priests supposed to trust in God, and be without fear? He didn't know very much about it, but that was what he had heard. Apparently, these two didn't completely trust their God.

Their eyes followed him as he gravitated toward the blanket-covered bodies and took a look at them all. He found three men, all killed with arrows. From the look of the shafts, they had been killed by the Blackfeet. He didn't know any of the men.

He covered the bodies again and was about to walk away when he saw a fourth one. It was also covered with a blanket, but it had been placed away from the other three bodies. He walked to it and removed the blanket and found himself looking at a dead woman, a nun.

"That's Sister Mary," Sally said. "Or was."

Pike saw that she had been shot, and not killed by the Indians. He covered her and straightened up.

"What's your name?" he asked.

"Sally Kennedy."

"Well, Sally, do you think you can tell me what happened now?"

"Why?" she asked, looking at him suspiciously. "Why are you so interested?"

"Because maybe I can help."

"You already have," she said. "Why don't you just get on your horse and ride away now?"

Pike looked around at the camp. "I don't see any horses, any mules."

"The Indians took them."

"And your supplies?"

"They took those too."

"And you want me to just mount up and ride away?" he asked. "You and your people will be dead in a week."

"We'll manage."

"Yeah," Pike said, "like you were managing when I got here? Like those two are managing now?" He inclined his head toward the two younger priests.

"They're frightened."

"Aren't you?"

"Yes," she said, "but the Lord will provide for us."

"Maybe he already has."

She stared at him for a moment. "You mean, you want me to believe that he sent you?"

"It's possible, isn't it?"

"Are you a Christian, Mr. . . ."

"Pike."

"Mr. Pike? Are you?"

"No, ma'am."

"Do you believe in God?"

"Can't say that I do."

"Then how can you suggest that he sent you here?"

"I was speaking from your point of view, ma'am," he said, "not mine."

"Why'd you come here, anyway?"

"I'm here to meet a friend," Pike said. "We've used this campsite from time to time. So you see, I've got another reason to be here, so while I'm waiting, why don't you just tell me what happened?"

Sally hesitated. "All right, then . . . but I'll start from the beginning."

"Let's get some coffee going, then," Pike said. "This sounds like it's going to be a long story."

It wasn't, but Pike found it engrossing nevertheless.

When the arrow pierced the chest of Nolan, Glory screamed, and the other men sprang into action. Dolan and Mallory ran for their guns, but were cut down in their tracks by a hail of arrows. The wooden shafts seemed to simply spring from their backs, and they fell to the ground dead—or so everyone thought.

"Stand still!" Father Smets shouted to Glory and

Sally. "Don't move at all!" He looked at the two younger priests, and they froze.

Both women obeyed him without question, and Sally admitted to Pike that she feared at that moment for her own life, and felt she was not ready to die.

"I started saying the act of contrition."

"The what?" Pike asked.

"Never mind," she said, and went on with her story.

While Father Smets, Glory, Sally, and the others stood fast, Indians came from out of the darkness into camp. There were about a dozen of them, Sally said, and they were painted. Once it was clear that they weren't going to be killed, Sally had visions of being raped by savages. That, however, was not destined to happen.

"The leader—at least I think he was the leader—seemed to find Father Smets more interesting than Glory and myself. He walked up to Father and began to study him. He touched his clothes, he even leaned close and sniffed him. Just at that moment, I saw Dolan. . . ."

Dolan, miraculously still alive even with four or five arrows in him, had crawled to his rifle and was now pointing it, apparently at the leader of the Indians.

"Look out!" Father Smets shouted, and as he pushed the Indian brave out of the way, Dolan fired. The ball struck Father Smets, and two Indians turned and let loose arrows that pierced Dolan's body and finally killed him.

Father Smets fell to the ground, and both Glory and Sally knelt over him.

"The leader, he just stared down at us, then turned and said something to the other Indians. After that, they all just . . . left."

"Their leader probably appreciated what your Father Smets had done for him," Pike explained.

19

"Then why didn't he help us nurse him?"

Pike grinned.

"The Indians around here are not nurses, Miss Kennedy, they're warriors," Pike explained. "You're lucky they *did* what they did and left Father Smets alive and . . ."

"And what?"

Pike hesitated. "And didn't take you with them and make squaws out of you."

"Squaws!" she said, her eyes widening.

"Indians aren't known for wasting strong young women, Miss Kennedy, and you and your friend—Glory?—are certainly both."

Sally looked as if she wasn't sure whether or not she had just been complimented.

"Coffee's ready," Pike said. "I've got some bacon in my saddlebags. Why don't you check on Father Smets and I'll start it cooking."

"You cook?"

"Do you find that unusual?"

"Well . . . I suppose not," she said. "I just thought—well, you are a mountain man, aren't you?"

"I prefer to think of myself as a man of the mountains," Pike said, "but either one describes me, I guess. Anyway, I'm very used to cooking for myself."

"You don't—you're not married?"

Pike thought briefly of the Crow woman, Sun Rising. "No, I'm not married," he said.

Sally stood up. "I'll just check on Glory and Father Smets." She started away, then stopped and turned. "Thank you for your help—I don't even know your name."

"It's Pike, ma'am," he said. "Jack Pike . . . and you're welcome."

TWO

While Pike and the two priests ate, Sally took her plate and one for Glory and went into Father Smets' tent. This left the two priests alone with Pike, which seemed to make them uncomfortable.

"I'm curious about something," Pike said to them.

"What?" one of them asked.

"If the Indians had meant to kill you," he said, "would you have fought them?"

"We're not fighting men," the other said. "We're missionaries."

"I know that," Pike said. "But isn't it in all of us to fight to stay alive?"

The two priests exchanged a look, and neither of them seemed to have an answer.

"I was just curious," Pike said, and continued eating.

After a while he spoke up again. "Tell me about the men you hired as guides."

"They were after the women," Father Santini said.

"They would have raped them if the Indians hadn't come," Father O'Neil said.

"Surely," Father Santini said.

Pike thought about asking them what they would have done then, but decided against it. Why make them feel any more ashamed—and he felt that they *must* have felt ashamed of themselves, the way they were cowering together now. They were probably only able to look each other in the eye, and that just barely.

When they were done eating Pike collected their plates and cleaned them. When Sally returned he took the two plates from her and asked, "How is Father Smets?"

"He's conscious," she said, wiping her hands on her thighs. "He would like to see you."

"Sure," Pike said. "Lead the way."

He followed her to the tent and entered behind her. The pale, younger woman looked up at him from her position by the cot, and then moved away to give him room to approach.

Father Smets looked to be about ninety years old, but Pike was sure that he was in his sixties. His injuries, and the ordeal he'd gone through, made him look much older than he was.

"You are Mr. Pike?" the old man asked.

"That's right."

"God bless you, my son, for coming to our aid."

"I only did what anyone else would do," Pike said. "How do you feel?"

"Better," Father Smets said, "much better. In the morning I will be stronger."

"Did he eat anything?" Pike asked Sally.

"A little."

"I will eat more in the morning," the older man said. "Now I must rest."

"Yes," Pike said, "that's right, get your rest."

"Mr. Pike," Father Smets said, reaching out and taking hold of Pike's arm. Pike was surprised at the strength in the seemingly frail hand that gripped him. "Will you be staying with us?"

"At least until my friend gets here, yes," Pike said.

The old man tried a smile and said, "We will talk tomorrow."

"Sure," Pike said, taking the man's hand from his arm and laying it back on the cot, "tomorrow."

Pike nodded to Glory, who resumed her position seated next to the cot. He stepped outside with Sally.

"He's a strong man," Pike said. "He'll make it."

"Thanks to you."

She seemed to have entirely changed her attitude toward him.

"Pike, when Father Smets is well we're going to have to move on," she said. "We'll have to find someplace to buy supplies, and find a new guide. Would you—"

"I'm really not much of a guide," he said.

"No, I was only going to ask if you would stay with us long enough to see us to safety. As you said before, alone we will probably perish. I realize that now."

"My friend will be here in a day or two," he said. "We can talk about it then."

"All right . . . but you'll stay with us that long?"

"Sure," Pike said. "At least that long, but I really only had enough supplies myself for one person for a few days. We'll have to ration the food and coffee."

"And water?"

"There's plenty of water around," he said, "and I might even be able to find us some game."

"Then we're in no imminent danger of . . . dying? Of freezing, or starving?"

"No," Pike said, "there's no danger of that."

"Again, thanks to you."

Pike was starting to find her gratitude a bit cloying.

"We're in your hands, Pike," Sally said. "Tell us what to do."

"Well," he said, "for starters, you can get those two men away from the fire and tell them to collect some more firewood."

"All right."

"After that I'll want to set a watch. They will rotate with me while you and Glory stay inside the tent with Father Smets."

"One of us can stay inside with him, while the other sleeps."

"That's what I want you to do," he said, "alternate watching him, but I want you both to stay inside the tent all night."

"I know it's warmer inside, but—"

"That's not it," Pike said. "I don't want any other Indians happening by and getting interested in you and Glory. I want you both out of sight as much as possible."

"I see," she said. "All right, I'll make sure Glory understands."

"Good," Pike said. "Those two, what are their names?"

"Fathers Santini and O'Neil."

"Let's get them moving."

"I don't think they're going to be much help to us," she said. "I mean . . . they haven't been so far."

"Well," he said, "that's going to change right now."

Once Sally explained to the two young priests that Pike was not only going to be staying in camp awhile, but that he was in charge, they came out from beneath their blankets and did what they were told. They collected enough wood to keep the fire going all night, and then listened as Pike explained the watch schedule. he would go first, then wake Father Santini, who would then wake Father O'Neil when it was his turn.

"Who do *I* wake?" Father O'Neil asked.

Pike studied him for a moment to see if he was serious. "Wake me at first light," he said, and Father

O'Neil nodded, satisfied that the drill would be complete.

"What are we watching for?" Father Santini asked.

Pike gave him a look similar to the one he had just given Father O'Neil.

"Trouble, Father," Pike said slowly. "We're watching for trouble."

"What kind of trouble?" Father O'Neil asked.

"You'll know it when you see it, Father," Pike assured him, "and when you do, wake me up right away. Understand? Even if you're not sure of what you see, wake . . . me . . . up."

They both indicated that they understood. Pike hoped that they did.

"All right, then. Roll yourselves up in your blankets by the fire and get some sleep. I'll wake Father Santini when it's his turn."

They nodded, and went to bed down by the fire.

Pike walked over to the tent and stuck his head in. Sally was sitting by Father Smets' cot, while Glory had covered herself with a blanket on the floor.

"Everything all right?" Pike asked.

"Yes," Sally said, "everything is fine . . . now."

Pike had been on watch a couple of hours when Sally came out of the tent. She had a blanket around her shoulders, and was using it to cover her hair. Obviously, she had taken what he'd said about staying out of sight of the Indians to heart. He wondered if he should tell her that there was nothing she could do to cover her hips, or her butt, or the proud thrust of her breasts. He decided not to mention it. It probably wasn't proper conversation in a missionary camp.

"What's wrong?" he asked as she joined him. "Is Father Smets all right?"

"He's asleep," she said.

"And Glory?"

"She's watching him."

"You should get some sleep then."

"I can't sleep," she said simply. "May I sit here with you for a little while?"

"Sure."

He was sitting on a boulder that was large enough for both of them, so he moved over to make room. She sat with her hip against his, and he decided that it was just an accident.

"When do you expect your friend to get here?" she asked.

"Actually," he said, "I thought he'd be here before me. He'll probably be along tomorrow."

"Will Father Smets be strong enough to travel by then?" she asked.

"If Skins—that's my friend, Skins McConnell—if he gets here tomorrow, we'll stay here another night and then see how the father—I mean Father Smets—feels."

"We all refer to him as Father."

"Even the other priests?"

"Yes," she said. "Of course, we call *them* Father, as well."

"It sounds confusing to me."

"It isn't, really," she said. "When any of us call Father Smets 'father' there's never any confusion. I guess we can just tell by the tones of our voices that we're referring to him."

Pike understood respect, and how it could be reflected in the tone of someone's voice.

Sally turned and looked over at the other two "fathers" sleeping by the fire.

"When will you be waking one of them for his turn?" she asked.

"I won't be."

"I thought you said—"

"I know what I said," he replied, cutting her off, "but I've decided that I really don't want to trust my life to them. They're too far out of their element." Pike added the last, not wanting her to think he was being disrespectful to men of the cloth.

"I understand," she said, hearing the awkwardness in his voice. "They really haven't been very helpful since we left the East."

"That's something I haven't found out yet."

"What?"

"Why you left the East?" he said. "Why are all of you here?"

"Well," she said, "the rest of us are here because we wanted to follow Father Smets."

"And why is Father Smets here?"

"Father wants to find the Flathead Indians."

"Why?"

"He wishes to study them, to learn how they live, what medicines they use."

"Why the Flathead?"

"Well," she said, "another band of missionaries came in search of them over a year ago, and we never heard from them again. That's another reason we're here, to find out what happened to them."

"Do you think they're dead?"

"Perhaps," she said. "Or perhaps they've been living with the Flathead Indians all these years."

"Well," Pike said, using his little finger of his right hand to scratch an itch in his ear, "the Flatheads are a little less savage than some of the other mountain tribes."

"Then the Indians who attacked us were not Flathead?" she asked.

"No," he said. "I saw the arrows in the bodies. Those Indians were from the Blackfoot tribe."

27

"A savage tribe?"

"Yes," he said, "towards whites, and towards the Flathead."

"They fight each other?" she asked. "How odd."

"Why odd?" he asked. "Don't white men fight white men?"

"Of course they do," she said, ducking her head. "It was a silly remark for me to make."

"Not silly," he said. "Just uninformed."

"How long have you lived in the mountains, Mr. Pike?"

"Just Pike, please," he said.

"Call me Sally."

"I've lived here a long time, Sally," he said. "Twenty years or more."

"You weren't born here?"

"No," he said, "I came from the East as a young man."

"Alone?"

"Yes."

"Do you still have family in the East?"

"No," he said. "When I left, they were all dead."

"And here?" she asked. "Do you have family here?"

"No," he said, shaking his head. "Just friends."

"Like Skins?"

"No, not like Skins," he answered. "Skins is . . . well, I don't have any other friends like him."

"You sound as if you are very close."

"We are," he said, and she could see that the subject made him uncomfortable, so she dropped it.

"You'd be better off if you tried to get some sleep," he said. "In the morning I'll go out and see if I can hunt up some food. Meanwhile, you make the last of the coffee and bacon for everyone else."

"Aren't you going to get some sleep?" she asked, standing. He felt a draft where the warmth of her hip had been.

"Not tonight."

"And you're giving us the last of your food," she said. "You're a good and charitable man, Pike."

"We usually help each other out up here, Sally," he said. "The mountains can be a harsh place to live. There aren't many of us who can survive up here alone."

"Like you?"

"Well," he said, "I've had a lot of practice surviving alone."

She looked as if she wanted to ask more questions, but she simply said, "Well, good night," turned, and walked back to the tent.

THREE

When first light came Pike woke both of the young priests, who started up confused and frightened. Pike knew they would have been no help on watch. He was right not to have awakened them for their turns.

"Get the coffee started," Pike said to them. "I'm going to see if I can't catch us some food."

They were both reaching for the coffee pot when he hefted his rifle and walked off to see if he could find any game.

This area of the Green River was usually fine for hunting, but for some reason he came across nothing that morning. The only reason he could think of for that was that the game had been frightened away. By what? A hunting party of Indians? Or a bear?

He went down to the river's edge and used his knife to cut a tree branch into a sharpened spear. He waded out into the river and managed to pierce two fair-sized fish. He hoped that the missionaries wouldn't be particular about what they had for breakfast.

When he returned to camp he saw that Sally was just starting the coffee.

"I told them to do that an hour ago," he said, giving the young priests an annoyed look. Neither of them was able to meet his eyes.

"They don't know how, Pike," Sally said. "It's all right. I've started the coffee. I was about to cook the bacon."

"Put these in the pan with it," he said, handing her the fish. "Do you know how to clean them?"

"Of course."

"Good," he said. "Don't waste the heads by cutting them off and throwing them away. We don't have that much to go around."

"Are you annoyed with me?" she asked, unsure of herself.

"No," he said, "I'm annoyed with them." He jerked his head toward the two priests.

"Don't be," she said. "They can't help themselves."

"They may be priests, but they're also men," Pike said contemptuously, then softened his tone when he saw her hurt look. "How is Father Smets this morning?" he asked.

"He's awake," she said. "Glory is inside with him."

"I'll check on him," he said. He started away, then turned and put his hand on her arm. "I'm sorry to take it out on you."

"That's all right," she said, smiling brightly. "I'll start breakfast."

Pike walked to the tent and entered. Glory looked up at him from her kneeling position next to the cot. Father Smets lifted his head from the pillow to see who she was looking at. That was encouraging. He hadn't been able to do that the day before.

"How are you feeling this morning?" Pike asked. He was going to call the priest "father," but found it difficult.

"I'm feeling much better," Father Smets said. "Much stronger."

"That's good." Pike looked at the girl, who he didn't think he'd ever spoken to directly, and said, "Why don't you go and help Sally with breakfast, Glory?"

The girl gave Father Smets a worried look.

"Go on, child," he said. "I'll be fine. Mr. Pike will be with me."

Glory got to her feet and slipped past Pike out of the tent.

"When may we get under way?" Father Smets asked.

"To where?" Pike asked.

"Well . . . I don't know. What is our situation?"

"You have no food, no supplies, and no horses or mules."

"Then we must go somewhere we can restock. Is there anyplace nearby?"

"Not nearby," Pike said, "but there are a couple of settlements you could go to."

"Would you take us there, Mr. Pike? I know you've done enough for us, but—"

"Don't worry," Pike said, holding up his hand. "I've already promised Sally that I would take you someplace where you could rest and buy more supplies—but I also told her that I wouldn't hire out as a guide."

"That's . . . acceptable," Father Smets said. "By the time we reach a settlement you will have done more than your share for us. We are greatly appreciative. God bless you."

"Yeah, well . . ." Pike said uncomfortably. "I'll see about breakfast and send one of the women in."

"Mr. Pike."

Pike turned as he was about to leave. "Just Pike, please," he said.

"Pike . . . why did you send Glory away? Did you

have something you wanted to talk to me about?"

Why *had* he sent her away?

"There are three dead men outside... Father Smets," Pike said, having difficulty addressing the man.

"You haven't buried them?"

"The ground's too hard. We'll just have to leave them. "But I *can* do something for the... other body."

The priest assumed a pained look. "Sister Mary."

"Yes."

"I would appreciate it, Pike, if you *could* do something to keep... animals from getting to her."

"I'll take care of it today," Pike said. "Those other two priests, they're not much good for anything, are they?"

Father Smets tried to smile. "Try not to be too harsh on them, Pike. They've come all this way with me when right from the beginning they were frightened."

"Sally has more guts than either of them."

"Sally has more courage than almost anyone I know," Father Smets said.

"Still... when I take care of Sister Mary's body, I'll send Sally and Glory in here with you, and make the other two help me."

"If you would send Fathers Santini and O'Neil in to see me," Father Smets said, "I will make certain that they know who is in charge. They will do anything you tell them to."

"All right," Pike said, "I'll send them in." He saw that the old priest looked tired and added, "Later, after breakfast."

"Yes," Father Smets said faintly, "later."

Pike went outside and instead of speaking to the two

priests talked to Sally.

"I'll have them go in and see him later," she assured him.

The smell of the bacon and fish and the odor of coffee made Pike's stomach growl, but he made sure that the others had had enough to eat before he joined them. As it turned out, Sally had saved him a fair-sized portion.

"Thank you," he said as she handed it to him, "but make sure the others have eaten—"

"We've all had our share," she said, "and I'm saving a little for Father Smets. You go ahead and eat."

He did. The flavor of the bacon did not exactly complement that of the fish, but it was better than nothing, and he finished it all. He washed it down with a cup of coffee, and then had another when Sally brought it to him.

"Was there no game to be found?" she asked, taking his empty plate from him.

"No," he said, deciding to be honest with her. "Something must have spooked them."

"Like what?"

"Could be anything," he said. "A band of Indians, or whites in the area; maybe the presence of a larger critter."

"Larger?"

"Maybe a bear."

"A bear?"

"Shh," he said. "I'm telling you because I feel I can talk to you. The others are more likely to panic."

"I understand," she said, and he could see that she was steeling herself. "I won't worry them with this . . . information."

"It's not information, Sally," he said. "It's just a guess."

"All right."

"Sally, can any of you use a gun?"

"I don't think the others can," she said, "but I can."

"Really?"

She smiled at him. "I haven't always been a missionary, Pike."

"Can you use a pistol?"

"Yes."

"I'll have to take it from one of the dead men. Can you handle that?"

She swallowed hard. "Yes."

"Good girl," Pike said. "Until Skins gets here, Sally, I need someone I can count on."

She smiled again, bravely. "You can count on me."

"I know I can," he said. He took her hand and squeezed it. "I know I can."

FOUR

As the day moved on into afternoon Pike decided to try hunting again.

He and the two young priests had managed to bury Sister Mary beneath a pile of rocks so that the animals wouldn't get at her. Pike didn't bother mentioning that sooner or later the larger animals would find their way to her anyway. He decided to let Sally and the others believe Sister Mary's body was now safe from scavengers.

He did no better hunting in the afternoon than he had in the morning. Something was still out there, spooking the game. He wasn't sure what he would have preferred, human varmints like the Crow or Blackfoot Indians, or animals like the bear or wolf.

He was heading back to camp on foot when he heard something. Someone or something was moving toward him from the opposite direction. He took cover behind a clump of rocks and held his rifle ready. The sound came closer and he identified it as that of a horse—just one—and from the sound of it, a shod horse, which left out Indians.

It had to be a white man.

As the rider came into sight he saw that it was indeed

a white man, but not just any old one.

Pike stepped from hiding and the man on horseback started for a moment, reaching for his rifle, before his eyes registered recognition and he stopped.

"Damn your eyes," Skins McConnell said. "You nearly scared me half to death."

McConnell got down from his horse and the two men shook hands warmly.

"You don't look like the past few months have been too hard on you," McConnell said. "If anythin', you look thinner."

"I may have dropped a few pounds," Pike said, patting his flat stomach. "You look good, too, Skins. What've you been up to?"

"You wanna talk about that here?" McConnell asked. "Or can we go someplace and have a cup of coffee?"

"We can go someplace," Pike said, "but you might be surprised at what you find there."

"Uh-oh," McConnell said. "I knew it. You've managed to find trouble already, haven't you?"

"More like it found me."

Shaking his head, McConnell said, "All right, tell me about it."

"Let's walk back to camp and I'll fill you in on the way."

By the time they reached camp McConnell had been caught up on everything that had happened.

"I don't know how you do it," he said to Pike.

"Do what?"

"Find trouble, and women—two women yet! Are they young *and* pretty?"

"Yup."

"Well, that's somethin', anyway. So we're gonna

have to lead them to a settlement and keep them safe without any help from the other men?"

"That's it."

"Sounds like fun."

"So what?" Pike said. "Your life has probably been dull the last few months anyway."

"Well, it's never dull when I'm around you, that's for sure."

As they entered camp Sally was at the fire with Fathers Santini and O'Neil. She gave McConnell a curious look, and both Pike and McConnell noticed the quiet looks of terror that crossed the faces of the two priests.

"Do they think I bite?" McConnell asked.

"Just don't make any sudden moves in their direction," Pike said.

They moved to the fire and Pike said, "Sally, this is my friend Skins McConnell."

"Hello," Sally said. "We're glad to see you."

"I can see why," McConnell said. "My friend here just came back from hunting empty-handed. I've got some bacon and dried beef."

"And coffee?" Sally asked.

"Yep."

"Good," she said, "I just used the last of Pike's."

"Father Santini," Pike said, "would you take care of Skins' horse?"

"Oh," Father Santini said, "of course."

"Father O'Neil," Pike said, "would you get the supplies from his saddlebags?"

"Uh, oh, yes, of course."

The two priests walked off with McConnell's horse, while Sally handed Pike and McConnell a cup of coffee.

"I'll help them get the supplies, and I'll start some lunch," Sally said.

"I see what you mean about those two," McConnell said.

"Sally says she can shoot, so I've got a pistol for her."

"From where?"

"One of the dead men."

"We ought to take their possible, too."

"I have, and their rifles. You never know when you might need an extra."

"And we've needed an extra plenty of times."

"Speaking of which," Pike said, "did you notice any game out there?"

"No," McConnell said. "As a matter of fact, it was too quiet and deserted."

"I know."

"Where are those extra rifles?" McConnell asked. "Let's make sure they're loaded."

"They're over by my bedroll," Pike said. "You see to them. I'm going to check on Father Smets."

"Will he be strong enough to travel tomorrow?" McConnell asked.

"We'll probably have to wait until tomorrow to find that out," Pike said.

He walked to the tent and went inside. Father Smets' eyes were open, and he appeared to be alert. Glory was sitting next to his cot.

"Pike," Father Smets said, "would you tell this young lady that it is all right to leave my side to go outside and get some air?"

"It's all right," Pike told her.

"But—"

"Go," Father Smets said.

Glory looked at them both and left.

"I do not want those two women hovering over me," Father Smets said.

"You know them better than I do," Pike said. "Tell them."

"I will," Father Smets said.

"How are you feeling?"

"Much better."

He looked better. There was more color in his face than there had been even earlier that same day.

"Has your friend arrived yet?"

"He just got here," Pike said. "We'll have some food for you in a moment."

"And some coffee?"

Pike nodded. "And some coffee."

"And I would like to get started early in the morning," Father Smets said. "It is imperative that we keep moving."

Unsettled by the eerie quiet that had surrounded them, Pike said, "I couldn't agree more, Father Smets."

Pike left the old priest alone in the tent and went back outside.

"You left him alone?" Glory asked when he reached the fire, obviously alarmed.

"He's fine, Glory," Pike said. "He's a tough old bird."

She gave him a dirty look.

"I didn't mean any disrespect," he said, looking at both her and Sally, who smiled at his discomfort.

Sally put her hand on Glory's arm. "It's all right, Glory. I think what Pike means is that he likes Father Smets."

"Right," Pike said, "right, that's exactly what I meant."

Glory gave him a doubtful look, but seemed to accept Sally's explanation. Pike walked over to where McConnell was sitting, watching the proceedings without much interest.

"This isn't exactly what I had in mind for our

reunion," McConnell said.

"What did you have in mind?"

"Well, I did have in mind two women," he said, "although not exactly these kinds of women."

"What kind are these kind?" Pike asked. "They're pretty."

"They're pretty enough," McConnell said, then leaned closer to Pike and said, "but missionary women, they don't . . . you know."

"Oh, I don't know," Pike said, turning his head to watch Sally. "I'm willing to bet that one of them has . . . 'you know' . . . once or twice in her life."

It was at that point that Pike realized that, given time and in another place, he would be attracted to Sally. She was reasonably self-assured for someone who was totally out of her element, and she was smart. She obviously hadn't gone into the missionary business for want of something better to do. He hoped that he would have time to get some background on her—and get to know her a little better in the "biblical" sense—before they parted company. What he *didn't* want to do, however, was get drawn into their "mission," which he suspected was more to civilize the Flathead Indians than it was to get to know them and their way of living.

"What are they doin' out here, anyway?" McConnell asked, breaking into Pike's reverie.

He told McConnell what Sally had told him about the Flathead Indians.

"That's crazy," McConnell said when he was finished. "I know the Flathead aren't as warlike as the Crow, the Blackfoot, even the Snake, but white men should leave Indians alone."

"Lunch is ready!" Sally called out to them.

"Let's go and eat," Pike said. "We're likely to run out of food before we reach a settlement."

"Where are we gonna take them?"

"Bonneville's Fort."

"There are a couple of places closer," McConnell pointed out.

"But none bigger," Pike said. "And Sandy Jacoby is in Bonneville's Fort."

"Oh," McConnell said, as if he suddenly understood why Pike wanted to go there. He smiled at his friend.

"It's not that," Pike said. "Sandy's a nurse, the closest thing to a doctor in these parts. She can have a look at Father Smets."

"Well, sure," McConnell said as they walked to the fire to have their lunch. "I knew that was the reason."

FIVE

That night, McConnell took the first watch, because Pike hadn't slept the previous night. This McConnell found out not from Pike but from Sally.

"You tryin' to kill yourself?" McConnell asked his friend.

"I'm trying to keep *from* being killed," Pike said. "I wasn't about to leave my life in the hands of those two."

"I notice you usually refer to Father Santini and Father O'Neil as 'those two.'"

"I don't like them," Pike said. "Just because they're priests doesn't mean they're not men."

"And you don't think they're actin' like men?"

"I think they're acting like frightened men."

McConnell gave his friend an amused look. "And you've never been frightened?"

Pike thought that over while he rolled himself up in his blanket, but it didn't occupy him for too long; sleep overtook him quickly.

While McConnell was on watch, Glory came out of the tent and went to the fire.

"Would you like some coffee?" she asked him. They were the first words he'd heard her speak.

"Sure, thanks."

She poured him a cup and carried it to him. She was wrapped in a blanket, which covered her head. As she handed McConnell the coffee he noticed that her skin was so fine he could plainly see the blue veins on the back of her hand. He found himself wondering if he'd be able to see the veins on her breasts as well. Maybe even follow them with his tongue . . .

"I'm sorry," he said, "did you say somethin'?"

"Your friend Pike," she said. "He's very . . ."

"Big?"

"Frightening."

"Why don't you sit awhile?" he asked. He was sitting on the same rock Pike had shared with Sally the night before. "I could use the company." When Glory sat next to him their hips did not touch.

"What's so frightening about Pike?" he asked.

"I don't know," she said, huddling inside the blanket. "He just frightens me. Yes, he's big, but he's also . . . forceful."

"You don't like forceful men?"

"My father was forceful," she said. "He used to . . . beat me a lot before he . . . died."

"Does Pike remind you of your father?"

"In a way, yes."

"What about the men who were guiding you?"

"What about them?"

"Did they frighten you?"

"Yes."

"And the Indians who killed them?"

"Yes," she said, "they did, too."

"Have you spent most of your life being frightened?" he asked.

She smiled wanly. "I suppose I have."

He noticed that her eyes were a very deep, dark blue, a color he didn't think he had ever seen before. He found himself drawn to them.

"It's only since I joined the church that I haven't been frightened," she said. "Up until this trip, that is."

"And why is that?" McConnell asked. "Isn't Father Smets forceful?"

"Oh, yes, but in his own way," she said. "I mean, he'd *never* use his hands—"

"From what I was told," McConnell said, "I think he might have if he had been given the chance the other night. I mean, when those other men were tryin' to—"

"No," she said. "No, Father would *never* use his hands." Her tone was very insistent. "Never!"

"All right," he said. "All right, never."

"I better go back," she said, standing. "He might need me."

"Thanks for the coffee," McConnell said.

"You're welcome."

She turned to leave and he called her name.

"Yes?" she answered, not turning to look at him.

"Do you find me frightening?"

She hesitated a moment, then said, "Oh, no," and hurried to the tent.

Well, he thought, that's somethin'.

When McConnell woke Pike, he gave him a negative report.

"I didn't see or hear a thing."

"I don't like the sound of that," Pike said.

"I know," McConnell said, "not even a bird."

"It's got to be an animal," Pike said. "A bear."

"Or a wolf."

"Right."

"Maybe a big cat?"

"Maybe."

McConnell laid down and wrapped himself up in his blanket.

"Keep your eyes and ears open," he said to Pike. "There should be some coffee left."

"Thanks."

"See you in a few hours."

Pike poured himself a cup of coffee, lifted his rifle, and went over to the rock they were using to sit on during watch. He would like to have wakened the two priests and made them sit and take a turn, but he still felt that he didn't want to put his life in their hands.

In fact, he so disliked them, that if *he* was a Catholic, he didn't think he'd even want to put his *soul* in their hands.

When morning came Pike woke McConnell first.

"I'm going to check on Father Smets," he said. "If he feels up to it, I think we'd better get moving this morning."

"Right," McConnell said. "I'll be ready."

"Get those two up," Pike said, and headed for the tent. He was surprised when, before he could reach it, the flap was thrown back and Father Smets stepped out, supported by Sally and fussed over by Glory. Pike was mildly surprised to find that the priest was almost as tall as he was.

"Good morning," Pike said.

"Morning, Pike."

"How are you feeling?"

"Fine."

"Fine?"

"Well . . . not fine, but well enough."

"Can you sit a horse?"

"I believe so."

"We have two," Pike said. "You'll ride one, Father. Sally, you and Glory will share the other one."

"Where will you be taking us?" Father Smets asked.

"A place called Bonneville's Fort. It might take us about three days to get there, but it's a fairly large settlement, and they have a nurse."

"That sounds fine," Sally said.

"Father, maybe you should wait another day," Glory said.

"No, child," Father Smets said, studying Pike's face. "I think Mr. Pike would like to get going today, and I wholeheartedly agree. We should move on."

Pike turned to look at McConnell, who had guessed what was going on and waved.

"Skins will saddle the horses," Pike said, "and then I'll help you into the saddle."

"Sally, perhaps you and Glory should help in breaking camp," Father Smets said.

"Can you stand all right?" Sally asked.

"If I can't I'd better find out now," he said. "Go on, both of you."

Sally let the priest's arm drop from her shoulders, and she and Glory reluctantly moved away.

"There's a problem," Father Smets said, looking at Pike's face.

"It's just too quiet, and I want to get started."

"Pike, why don't you call me Adrian?"

"Adrian?"

"It's my first name," Father Smets said, "and I believe you'll have less trouble with it than you are having with 'father.' Or perhaps you'd rather call me Smets?"

"Uh . . . no . . . Adrian should be fine."

"When I was a boy," Father Smets said, "my father used to call me 'Andy.'"

"Andy," Pike said. That seemed the easiest of all.

"You may use it if you like."

"All right, Andy," Pike said. "All right."

"Good," Father Smets said. "That's settled, now

49

maybe we can see about getting me up on that horse, hmm?"

They broke camp, and Pike and McConnell lifted Father Smets up onto Pike's horse, while McConnell helped Glory onto his.

"We're going to walk?" Father Santini asked. Father O'Neil looked equally aghast at the notion.

"Do you have another idea?" Pike asked him. He included Father O'Neil in his look.

"Well . . . no . . . but . . ." Father Santini looked at Father O'Neil helplessly, and the other man returned the glance.

"Walking won't kill you, Father," Father Smets said to Santini.

"Father Santini," Pike said, "you bring up the rear with McConnell. Father O'Neil, you lead Glory on the horse." Sally had already volunteered to lead Father Smets' horse, and Pike agreed. He would take the lead, alone. If there was going to be trouble, he didn't want anyone in his way when it came time to move.

Pike wondered why he had no trouble referring to the other two priests as "father." Perhaps it was because he didn't respect them enough for it to be a problem—and as much as he disrespected them, he was awed by Father Smets.

"All right, then," Pike said, "let's get moving. I'm going to keep up a pretty good pace, so anyone who gets tired better sing out."

Somehow, he was sure he knew which two of the group would be the first to do so.

SIX

They walked until—as Pike had expected—Father Santini and Father O'Neil began to complain of fatigue.

"We can't stop now," Pike said the first time the two requested a rest.

The second time, he said, "The two of you could rest here and then catch up."

They stopped complaining after that.

They switched off at one point, Sally mounting McConnell's horse and Glory going on foot. At that point Pike made Father Santini lead Sally's horse, while Glory walked with McConnell.

Through the morning and into the afternoon Pike didn't see so much as a bird. If it was a bear that had scared the animals out of the area, it had to be a big one. He and McConnell had had plenty of experiences with bears, and he wasn't looking forward to any more.

Of course, they'd had numerous run-ins with Indians of every mountain tribe, and he wasn't looking forward to that, either. For a man who disliked trouble as much as Pike did, McConnell was right: either he managed to find it, or it managed to find him. This time they just seemed to both be going in the same direction. He was bound and determined to make sure that he and the missionaries went their separate ways once they reached Bonneville's Fort.

He thought briefly about Sandy Jacoby. She had nursed him back to health after the Blackfeet had killed the man he was hunting with and wounded him. He'd managed to walk all the way to Bonneville's Fort and arrived not only wounded but feverish. It was Sandy who kept him from dying, and after that they had become *very good* friends. It would be nice to see her again after so long.

He liked to think that no matter how bad a situation was, some good could come from it.

They didn't stop to rest until Father Smets showed the need to. To his credit, the old man never once asked, but Sally rode up on Pike as they were approaching mid-afternoon.

"Pike, Father Smets needs to rest."

Pike looked back and saw the old priest slumping in the saddle. He waved his arm at McConnell, indicating that they were going to stop.

He took his canteen and handed it to Sally, then walked back to Father Smets.

"Why are we stopping, Pike?" the old priest asked, looking down at him.

"I'm tired, Andy. Come on, let's get you down from there."

Pike helped Smets down to the ground, surprised again at how tall the man was, and how light he was for a man of his height.

"Let's find someplace to sit down." As he led Father Smets away he said to McConnell, "You want to water the horses?"

"Yeah," McConnell said, "you water the priest, and I'll water the horses."

He led Father Smets to a big enough rock and lowered him down to a seated position

"Here, drink some water."

"Let the others drink first," Father Smets said, pushing the canteen away.

"We have plenty of water," Pike said. "No one drinks until you do."

Father Smets stared at Pike, realized that he was serious, and took the canteen. While he sipped from it Pike examined his wound. He had been afraid that the priest might start bleeding again, but the wound was not even oozing. All they had to worry about now was the threat of infection. Hopefully, they'd reach Bonneville's Fort before anything like that could happen.

"How is he?" Sally asked.

"He looks fine," Pike said. "How do you feel, Andy?"

"I'm fine," Father Smets said breathlessly. He handed Sally the canteen and repeated, "I'm fine."

"A little tired, huh?" Pike asked.

"Why should I be tired?" he asked. "You and the horses are doing all the walking."

"Right," Pike said. "I'm just going to check on everyone else, and the horses. You sit here awhile, okay?"

"Fine," Father Smets said. "I'm fine."

"I know you are," Pike said, touching the man lightly on the shoulder.

He took the canteen from Sally and said, "Stay with him."

He walked over to where McConnell was letting his horse drink from his hat.

"Everyone get watered?" Pike asked.

"Last one," McConnell said, touching his horse's nose.

"You notice anything?"

"Like what?"

"Like maybe we're being followed?"

McConnell cocked his head for a moment. "No, I don't think so."

"No," Pike said, "I don't think so, either. Not by anything human, anyway."

"We'd hear something human," McConnell said.

It was unnerving, feeling that there was something out there, and not seeing or hearing anything, especially for men like Pike and McConnell. They had enough confidence in their own abilities to feel that if anything *was* following them—anything human—at the very least, *one* of them would know it.

"How long are we gonna be here?" McConnell asked.

"Not long enough to make new friends," Pike said. "I just want to give Father Smets some time to get his breath back."

"The two young priests are pretty breathless, too," McConnell said.

Pike looked over to where Fathers Santini and O'Neil were sitting on the ground, their heads bowed into their hands. They were either praying or they were too tired to hold their heads up.

"They'll live," Pike said. "We'll move on when Father Smets is ready."

"Who decides that?" McConnell asked. "You or him?"

Pike looked over to where Sally was crouched down next to Father Smets. "She does."

Pike remembered that he was the only one who

hadn't had some water and he took a swig and stoppered the canteen.

"There must be a stream nearby," McConnell said. "I'll take the canteens and refill them."

"All right," Pike said. "We'll be here long enough for you to do that."

"I'll take Glory with me."

Pike stared at his friend for a minute, then decided it was none of his business.

"Go ahead, then," he said. "Don't get lost."

McConnell shook out his hat and put it back on his head. He took the canteen from Pike and slung it over his shoulder with the other one. Pike watched him walk over to where Glory was standing staring at the ground, then turned and went back to Father Smets.

"Where are we going?" Glory asked.

"We're gonna get some more water for the canteens," McConnell said.

"Is it safe?" she asked worriedly.

"It's safe enough," he said. "Here, carry a canteen."

She took it and held it in both hands.

"They won't leave without us, will they?" she asked.

"No, they won't leave," he said. "Come on, don't be such a worrier."

"I can't help it."

McConnell knew that, but he also knew that he wanted to help her, if he could, in whatever time they had. Taking her with him to find the stream was just the first step.

"How do we find the stream?" she asked.

"Use your nose," he said. "You'll be able to smell it."

*   *   *

"How are you doing, Andy?" Pike asked Father Smets.

The older man looked up at him and smiled.

"I'm catching my breath, Pike," he said. "Isn't that what you had in mind?"

"I had it in mind for all of us to catch our breaths," Pike said. "Sally, how about you?"

"I'm fine," she said.

"Why don't you go and see how those other two are doing?"

She knew who he meant.

"All right."

As she walked away Father Smets said, "I am going to try to teach you to be more charitable towards others, Pike."

"I'm charitable," Pike said, as if stung by an accusation.

"I mean others who you don't particularly like."

"Oh, you mean like those two?"

"Yes," Father Smets said, "those two. If you gave them enough time, I'm sure they would manage to surprise you."

"Andy," Pike said sincerely, "the last thing I want right now is a surprise. I'd like the rest of this trip to be nice and predictable."

"You're still worried."

Pike looked down at the man. "I'm always worried about something, Andy. That's how come I've lived so long up here."

"What about Indians?"

"Actually," Pike said, "running into a few Indians right now wouldn't be such a bad thing."

"Why is that?"

"We could trade with them."

"For what?"

"Another horse would be a good start," Pike said. "Two ponies would be even better."

"What would you give them?"

"Andy," Pike said, "you came up here to deal with Indians. I'm sure you brought along a few little items."

"Well," Father Smets said, "we did bring rosary beads. Thank God those other Indians didn't find them the other night."

"Rosary beads," Pike said. He wasn't sure what they were, but they sounded like jewelry. "Well, Indians are pretty fond of jewelry. That might work."

"I'll have Sally get them." Father Smets started to rise, then sat back rather abruptly. "I guess I'm not all that ready to get up myself. Give me a hand, will you?"

"Not just yet," Pike said, putting his hand firmly on the priest's uninjured shoulder. "We don't need them right now. I'll tell you when."

Maybe never, he thought. But he knew one thing. They'd get a lot further trading beads with Indians than they would with a wild animal.

By the time McConnell and Glory returned with refilled canteens Sally had informed Pike that Father Smets seemed ready to move on.

"Your friend seems to have taken an interest in Glory," she added.

"I suppose," Pike said. "Does that bother you?"

"No," Sally said, "not at all—as long as he doesn't hurt her."

"Sally, I don't think Skins has any intention of hurting Glory."

"She's still very young," Sally said, "and very inexperienced."

"I thought you were all inexperienced," Pike said.

"In the mountains, yes," Sally said, "but some of us have lived other lives, Pike. We're not all as naive as Glory, or as timid as Fathers Santini and O'Neil."

"I've noticed that."

"You have?" she said, smiling. "Good."

Sally was becoming more and more interesting to him as time went by.

They had been traveling only about an hour when Sally suddenly ran up to join Pike.

"Father Smets wants to talk to you, Pike."

"Does he want to stop?"

"No," she said, "just go back and see him."

Pike followed her back to Father Smets, where he turned and began to keep pace with the priest's horse.

"You wanted to talk to me, Andy?"

"I want to try to put your mind to rest, Pike."

"About what?"

"This unusual quiet you seem so concerned about."

"What about it?"

"I only mean to point out," Pike said, "that it may not be something to worry about."

"What is it, then?"

"Well . . . I know you're not Catholic, but it could be the work of the Lord."

Pike stared up questioningly at Father Smets for a few moments. "You mean . . . he's clearing the way for us?"

"That's exactly what I mean."

Pike nodded and continued walking.

"How do you feel about that?"

"Well . . . it would be nice to believe that, Andy," Pike said. "I mean, it really would."

"But you can't?"

"I'd like to, is all I'm saying," Pike said. "I mean, it sure would put our minds at rest, wouldn't it?"

"At ease, perhaps," Father Smets said, "but I suspect not at rest."

Pike patted his horse on the neck. "I'll think about it, Andy."

"That's all I ask," Father Smets said, and Pike went back to the head of the column and did just that.

SEVEN

"He said *what?*" McConnell asked.

Because there were seven of them they built two campfires. One would already have given their location away to anyone who was interested, so two could not be any worse, and it would probably help. For one thing, Pike didn't have to sit at the same fire with Fathers Santini and O'Neil.

"He said he thought God was clearing the way for us," Pike said. "That's why we haven't see anyone along the way—animals or men."

They had already eaten dinner, and both Sally and Glory had taken Father Smets away, laid him down, and covered him with blankets to keep him warm. Because they were traveling largely on foot, they had left his tent behind, something Sally had argued against, though Father Smets had understood.

Pike and McConnell sat alone at one fire; the two young priests were at the other.

"And you believed him?"

"I didn't say I believed him."

"You let *him* think you believed him?"

"I said I'd think about it."

"Pike," McConnell said, "that's crazy."

"If we believed it," Pike said, "we wouldn't have to worry about it anymore, would we?"

"There ain't no God, Pike," McConnell said. "I mean, everybody talks about one and all, but I ain't never seen hide nor hair of him, have you?"

"We're not supposed to."

"You tellin' me you believe in God?" McConnell said. "After some of the things we seen? After what happened to Sun Rising? Come on, Pike!"

"I'll take the first watch," Pike said. He took his rifle, stood up, and walked away.

McConnell knew he had made a mistake mentioning Sun Rising. One of the reasons Pike had gone off alone was to deal with his feelings about what had happened to her, what he had done for revenge, and how it had affected him as a man afterward. McConnell had avoided asking Pike about it, and now he had gone and blurted it out.

He got up and followed his friend.

"Pike."

The big man turned and looked at him.

"I'm sorry for what I said back there," McConnell said. "About Sun Rising, I mean."

"It's all right," Pike said. "It really is, Skins; I'm over it."

"Still . . . it was a stupid thing to say."

"I've said my share of stupid things."

"Well, all right. I just wanted to apologize."

"Get some sleep," Pike said to his friend. "I'll wake you in a few hours."

McConnell nodded and went back to the fire.

Pike found it strange that the remainder of the trek to Bonneville's Fort was uneventful. They still hadn't seen any animals or Indians, and every time Pike looked at Father Smets he was reminded of what the priest had said. It was just coincidence, wasn't it?

"There's Bonneville's Fort," Pike said to Sally, who had been walking beside him for the last half day.

"It's big," she said. "I didn't expect to find any place that big in the mountains."

"It's grown since I was last here," Pike said. "More wooden buildings and less tents."

"It looks close from here," she said. "How far is it?"

"Should be another hour or so," Pike said. "We'll be there by nightfall."

"Good," she said. "Father Smets needs a lot of rest after this."

"I know."

"Pike," she said, "what do you think of what he said to you?"

"What do you mean?"

"You know what I mean."

"I haven't been thinking about it much, Sally," he said honestly.

"Why? Does it disturb you to think about God?"

"It's just not something I think a lot about."

"Maybe you should."

Pike looked at her. "I don't want to be part of your missionary work, Sally."

He thought the remark might hurt her feelings, but it didn't. Instead, she put her hand on his arm and looked him right in the eye.

"I don't want you to be."

"All right," he said after a moment. "Let's get Father Smets to where he can get all the rest he needs."

He turned, waved his arm, and they started down toward Bonneville's Fort.

Jean-Luc Kenyon had been the *booshway* of

Bonneville's Fort since the first tent was erected, and he was proud of the way the fort had developed over the years. Kenyon stood six feet, but his rock-hard paunch made him look shorter than that. He had the fullest beard anyone had ever seen, and in his early fifties he was still a feared man in a fight.

Kenyon was walking from the trading post to his horse when he saw a group of people entering the settlement. He recognized Pike immediately and felt a flush of pleasure at the sight of him. There were six people with the big man, and the only one he recognized was Skins McConnell.

"Damn, it's good to see you boys!" he said when they reached him. He shook each of their hands warmly and firmly. It had been over a year since he'd seen either of them.

"What brings you here this time?"

"We've got an injured man, Jean-Luc," Pike said. "A priest."

"In fact," McConnell said, "we've got three priests, and a couple of women."

"Missionaries?"

"Yup," Pike said.

Kenyon shook his head and said, "They keep comin', don't they?"

"There were missionaries here before?" Pike asked.

"Some, yeah," Kenyon said, "little over a year ago."

"I'm sure Father Smets will want to talk to you about it, Jean-Luc," Pike said, "but right now we'd like Sandy to take a look at him. That is, if she's still here."

"Sandy? Sure, she's here. She's gonna be real glad to see you. Come on."

Along the way Pike introduced the missionaries to Kenyon, and explained that he was the *booshway* of Bonneville's Fort. When they didn't understand the term, he told them it was like being the mayor. *That* they were able to understand.

As they approached the wooden structure that was the unofficial hospital of the fort the door opened and Sandy Jacoby stepped out. She was wearing a man's shirt, jeans, and boots, and her blond hair was shorter than it had been when Pike was last there. Obviously, she had heard them coming. When she recognized Pike, though, she leaped off the low porch with a whoop and ran into his arms.

"You cut your hair," was the first thing he said to her.

"That's the only thing about me that's changed," she promised, and then kissed him long and soundly.

"Sandy," he said when his mouth was free, "we have a patient for you."

"Who?"

"A man, a priest. He was shot. I got the ball out and stopped the bleeding, but—"

"When did it happen?" she asked, suddenly serious.

"About four days ago."

She squeezed his biceps and said grimly, "We'll continue this later. Let's him him inside."

Pike turned, but McConnell was already helping Father Smets down from the horse. Leaning on McConnell, both men followed Sandy inside. Pike turned and found Sally staring at him.

"Old friend of yours?" she asked.

"Not so old," he said, "but yeah, a friend."

She nodded shortly, and then followed the others into the building.

"Jean-Luc, could you show me where I can camp these people?"

"Sure," Kenyon said to him and the others, "come this way."

"Follow me," Pike said to Glory. He didn't speak

to Fathers Santini and O'Neil, but they followed anyway.

They found a campsite, and Pike made arrangements with Kenyon to bring the missionaries some supplies.

"Do you have a tent?"

"We can rustle one up."

"And someone to put it up for them?"

"Sure."

Pike turned to the two young priests. "Both of you stay here and wait for the supplies. I'm going to go and check on Father Smets."

"Can I come with you?"

Pike turned and looked at Glory in surprise. She'd spoken very few words directly to him in the past few days, preferring instead to talk to McConnell.

"Of course," he said. "Come on."

As Pike was leaving with Glory he heard Kenyon saying, "I'll have the supplies brought right over, Father—I mean, Fathers—I mean—"

Pike smiled.

When they reached Sandy's hospital, Pike opened the door and allowed Glory to precede him. The inside of the shack was separated into two small rooms. McConnell and Sally were waiting in the outer room while Sandy was obviously examining Father Smets in the other room.

"Any word?" he asked.

"No," Sally said. "Where are the others?"

Pike told her that they had found a campsite for them, and that Fathers Santini and O'Neil were now waiting for supplies.

"We can't pay much," Sally said.

"We'll work that out," Pike said.

Glory moved over to McConnell and sat next to him, her hands folded in her lap.

"I'll see to the horses," Pike said.

"I'll do that," McConnell said. He seemed anxious for a reason *not* to remain waiting. He stood up, and Glory did the same.

"I'll help," she said.

"Good," McConnell said. "We'll see you two later. Pike, I'll find us a spot."

"Fine," Pike said.

When McConnell and Glory had left, Pike looked at Sally. She seemed on the verge of collapse.

"Tired?" he asked.

"Exhausted."

"Sandy might have a place for you to lie down—" he started, but she cut him off.

"That won't be necessary," she said. "I don't want to distract her from Father Smets. I'll rest later, when we find out how he is."

As if on cue the door to the other room opened and Sandy stepped out. She left the door open. They could see inside the room. Father Smets was lying on a bed, a sheet covering him to his shoulders. His face seemed as white as the sheet. Pike remembered what he and Sally had done in that bed a year ago, and thought it ironic that a priest should now be lying in it.

"How is he?" Sally asked.

"Who removed the ball and bandaged him up?" Sandy asked. She had just washed her hands and was drying them on a towel.

"I did."

"I thought so," she said. "You did a nice clean job.

There's no infection."

"Thank God for that," Sally said, putting her hands together.

"I'd like to keep him here tomorrow, and then you can move him to a campsite."

"When will he be able to travel?" Sally asked.

"I'd like him to stay put for a couple of weeks," she said, "but in the end, that's going to be up to him. I've only known him a few moments, but already I can see that he's not the type to be able to stay still for too long."

"You're right about that."

Sandy turned to Pike. "What are your plans?"

"McConnell and I will probably stay around for a day or two, get outfitted and then ride out."

"A day or two, hmm?" Sandy asked. "We have some serious catching up to do, you know."

"Uh, I know," Pike said, trying not to look at Sally. "We can talk later."

"Talk," Sandy said. "All right. That's a start."

"I've got to get settled," Pike said, "and get a beer." He turned to Sally. "You should go and get some rest."

"I know," she said, "but—"

"Father Smets is in good hands," Sandy said, "even if I do say so myself. Would you like me to examine you, as well?"

"That won't be necessary," Sally said. "I just need some sleep."

"Make sure you get a lot of it," Sandy said, looking from Pike to Sally. Obviously, she was wondering if there was anything going on between them. There wasn't, but why was Pike feeling uncomfortable being in the same room with the two women?

"I'll talk to you later, Sandy," Pike said again. "Come on, Sally. I'll show you where your campsite is."

Pike allowed Sally to exit before him, then left without looking back.

"You don't have to waste your time with me, you know," Sally said when they were outside.

He wasn't quite sure what she meant by that. "I'm not wasting my time, Sally. I'll get you settled, and then see to getting myself settled."

"I don't want to be a bother," she said, "if you have something better to do."

"At the moment," he said, "I don't."

EIGHT

Pike took Sally to the campsite and left her with Fathers Santini and O'Neil. Kenyon had already had the supplies delivered, and a couple of men were there putting up a tent. Pike left it up to Sally to tell the other two priests about Father Smets' condition.

Pike went into the settlement and found the trading post, and next to it, a saloon and restaurant. Since McConnell was taking care of collecting the supplies, he went into the saloon. It was small, with a makeshift bar and only a few tables, one of which he sat at. The bartender greeted him by name. As hard as Pike tried, he couldn't remember the man's name, so he simply returned the greeting.

"What can I get for ya?" the bartender asked.

"How about a beer and a steak?"

"Comin' up."

While he waited he thought about Sally and Sandy and about Father Smets. He was sure that Father Smets would be able to find a guide in Bonneville's Fort. In fact, he himself might even be able to recommend somebody. He figured he and McConnell would stay on for a couple of days and then pull out. One of the things about being alone for so long was that he hadn't seen a woman in three months. For a while, he had thought that maybe he and Sally would . . . and then later, when they decided to come to Bonneville's Fort, he knew he'd be seeing Sandy. Now Sally and Sandy had met, and obviously didn't like each other, and this wasn't the kind of situation Pike had been looking forward to. It would have been a lot simpler if he hadn't met up with the missionaries, and if he and McConnell had just gone to a different settlement. Then all he would have had to do was visit a whore a couple of times, and that particular itch would have been scratched.

McConnell and Glory were next door in the trading post. McConnell was taking care of getting himself and Pike outfitted with enough supplies to last them a few weeks at least. They'd want to be out that long before they had to come back in for supplies.

"Where will you be going?" Glory asked.

"Huntin'," McConnell said, "trappin'."

"Hunting and trapping what?"

"Buffalo, maybe some elk. As far as the trappin' goes, it'll be beaver, but there just ain't as many beaver as there used to be."

"You kill these animals?"

"Well . . . of course."

"Then that explains why there aren't any more," she said. "You've killed them all."

"Well, *I* haven't, not all by myself," he said, trying to lighten the mood, but she wasn't having any of that.

"And how long will it be before the buffalo and the elk are gone?" she asked. "They're all God's creatures, Skins."

"Glory," he asked, "you eat meat, right?"

"No," she said.

He thought he had the perfect argument, but apparently that wasn't the case.

"You don't?"

"I can't," she said. "I can't eat animals."

He tried a different tack.

"Does Father Smets eat meat?"

"Well . . . yes, but he doesn't kill it."

"Then it's all right to eat it if you're not the one who killed it?"

"No, of course not."

"Then how does Father Smets explain it?"

"I—I've never questioned him about it."

"Why not?"

"Well," she said somewhat helplessly, "uh, because he's Father Smets."

"Well, I'll tell you what," he said. "After you've made him explain why he eats meat, I'll explain why I kill it *and* eat it. All right?"

"Well . . . all right."

He smiled to himself, thinking that he had handled that very well.

When they left the trading post he said, "Glory, I'm gonna go and find Pike so we can make some plans. Why don't you go back to the campsite."

"Maybe I'll go and see Father Smets—" she started, but he cut her off.

"I don't think that's a good idea," he said. "He's probably asleep, and if he's not, he probably shouldn't be talkin' to anyone."

"Oh, I won't talk to him. I'll just sit with him and pray."

"Look, why don't you just let me walk you back to the campsite?" he offered. "I'm sure Sally will have some information about Father Smets for you, and she's probably there already."

"Well, all right, if that's what you think is best."
"I do," he said. "Come on."

The front door of the saloon opened and McConnell walked in. He looked around, walked over, and sat down next to Pike.

"Where's Glory?"

"I took her to the campsite and left her with Sally. What did you do to *her?*"

"I didn't do anything to her," Pike said.

"She was in a foul mood."

"Well," Pike said, "she and the others have been through a lot."

"But with Father Smets in good hands at Sandy's, I figured they would be—oh, wait a minute. Sally met Sandy, right?"

"So?"

"And you're in a pretty foul mood, too," McConnell said, "aren't you?"

Pike looked past McConnell. "Well, if I am, this should go a long way to improve it."

McConnell looked behind him and saw the bartender approaching with Pike's steak and beer.

"Hi, Skins," the bartender greeted him.

"Hello, Al," McConnell said as the man put the food and drink down on the table. "I'll have the same."

"Comin' up."

Al, Pike thought. That was the man's name? It still didn't sound familiar. Maybe he had never known the man's name to begin with.

"After three months on your own, I guess you were lookin' forward to a woman, huh?"

"I was, yeah," Pike said, spearing a piece of the bloody meat.

"But not two, right? Didn't expect to get in this much

trouble so soon, did you?"

"No."

"You and women, Pike," McConnell said, shaking his head and laughing.

"Me and women?" Pike asked. "What about you and women? Glory isn't exactly your usual type, is she?"

McConnell grew serious.

"There's somethin' sad about her, don't you think?" McConnell asked. "She's scared all the time, and she don't talk much."

"She seems to like you well enough."

"I guess," McConnell said. "I know she's afraid of you."

"Afraid of me? What for?"

"You're so big and rough," McConnell said, his tone growing light again.

"Cut it out," Pike said gruffly. "Did you get all our supplies?"

"Yeah, and we're camped south of the settlement."

"Good," Pike said. The missionary camp was northwest of the settlement, while Sandy's place was northeast.

"How long are we intendin' to stay around here?" McConnell asked.

"I don't know," Pike said. "A couple of days I guess."

"We gonna end up guidin' the missionaries?"

"No!" Pike said quickly. "I might help them find a guide they can trust, but that's as far as I'll go. I'm lookin' to mind my own business."

Al returned with McConnell's steak and beer, and told them both to enjoy their meals.

"The missionary camp looks like it got outfitted pretty well," McConnell said.

"Kenyon took care of them."

"Sandy say how long Father Smets would be laid

up?" McConnell asked.

"She said how long she'd *like* to see him laid up. She knows as well as I do that old man ain't going to stay still for that long. By the end of the week he's going to want to be on the move."

"Well," McConnell said, pretending to be absorbed in his steak, "we won't have to worry about that, because we won't be here, right?"

"That's right," Pike said. "That's damn right!"

McConnell thought that perhaps Pike was protesting too much.

After they finished eating, Pike said he was going to go and see Sandy.

"Good luck," McConnell said.

"Now what's that mean?"

"It doesn't mean anything," McConnell said defensively. "All it means is good luck."

"I just want to check on Father Smets."

"Fine."

"And do some catching up with Sandy."

"Of course," McConnell said. "Hey, we have some catching up to do, too. I can understand that."

Pike stood up. "Then don't be giving me a hard time about it."

"I'm not gonna give you a hard time," McConnell said. "I promise."

Pike stared at his friend for a moment, then turned to leave.

"Uh, one thing," McConnell said.

"What?"

"Do you want me to start thinkin' about who would make a good guide for Father Smets and his missionaries?"

"Sure," Pike said, "why not? Find out who's in the

settlement, and who'd be a good guide."

"Okay," McConnell said. "I'll have another beer and then take care of it."

Pike started to leave again, then hesitated.

"Anything else?"

"No, nothing else."

"I know you, Skins," Pike said, pointing an accusing finger at his friend. "You've got something on your mind, something planned."

"I don't have anything planned, Pike," McConnell said, spreading his hands innocently. "I'm just gonna let nature take its course."

Pike nodded and started for the door, but when he got to it he suddenly turned and called out, "And what's *that* mean?"

Pike walked over to Sandy's and knocked on the door. He didn't feel that he had anything specific to apologize for, but he did feel that things were too awkward for their first meeting after almost a year, and he wanted to clear that up.

When Sandy opened the door and saw him she smiled. "I've been expecting you," she said.

"You have?"

"Uh-huh," she said, nodding. "Come on in."

He entered and she closed the door behind them and turned to face him.

"How is Father Smets?" he asked.

"Oh, he's doing just fine," she said. "He's asleep right now . . . but you didn't come back here to talk about him."

"I didn't?"

"No," she said, shaking her head and moving closer to him, "you didn't."

She slid her arms up around his neck and pulled his

face down to hers so she could kiss him. Her lips melted against his and the kiss went on for a very long time. He took her in his arms as their mouths opened and it became a lingering, searching kiss, and when it ended they were both out of breath.

"That's what you came back for," she said huskily. "That was your hello kiss."

"If that was my hello kiss," he asked, putting his big hands on her waist, "what comes next?"

"Wait," she said, releasing her hold on his neck and moving back out of his grasp. "Let me lock the door and I'll show you."

He thought she was talking about the outside door, but as he watched her she walked to the door separating the room they were in from the room Father Smets was in. She locked it, then turned to face him with her back to it.

"Now . . ." she said.

NINE

"Sandy," Pike said, "there's a priest in the next room."

"So?" she said, moving close to him again and speaking barely above a whisper. "We'll just have to be very, very quiet."

She pulled his shirt up out of his pants and slid her hands underneath, running them over his muscular chest. He pulled *her* shirt from her pants and slid his hands underneath, over the smooth, hot flesh of her back. They kissed again, and slid down to the floor together.

She had a small cabin out back, but he knew she wouldn't leave the building while she had a patient in bed—and the bed that Father Smets was in was the only one she had for patients. That left only one place for their lovemaking—the floor.

They eagerly removed each other's clothing. Pike, having been without a woman for three months, found himself filled with a desperation he hadn't experienced in quite a while. When she had his pants off she attacked his erect penis, using her hands and her mouth, and it was all he could do to keep from bursting right there and then. He gritted his teeth and held her head while she rode him with her sweet mouth. She still had her trousers on, and he pulled her legs around so that he could remove them without causing her to release him from her mouth. When he had them off, and her underwear, he ran his hands over her smooth thighs, then pulled her around farther still so he could press his face between her legs. He'd used his mouth on women before, but he had never done it when someone was attending to him in the same way, which only increased the excitement he was feeling. As he touched his tongue to her moist slit she started, moaned, and sucked on him harder. He delved into her sweet, hot depths with his tongue, taking hold of her buttocks with his big hands. He held her tightly and used his lips and tongue on her until she was so overcome that she had to release him to cry out.

She turned quickly and mounted him, driving herself down on him until he was completely engulfed. She leaned over him so that her beautiful breasts dangled in his face, and he took them in his hands and bit and sucked her nipples while she rode him. Finally, he could hold it back no longer and he exploded into her, biting his lip so that he wouldn't shout. As occupied as he was, he was still aware that there was a priest in the next room.

She began to bounce up and down on him so hard that he thought she was going to drive his lower back through the wooden floor. He reached for her and pulled her down to him so that her breasts were crushed against his chest. Her hungry mouth sought his and latched onto it, and her tongue blossomed sweetly in his mouth. Her insides seemed to be sucking his juices from him and he thought he would never stop ejaculating. It went on for so long that it became painful and exquisite at the same time. Her own passion had reached its zenith and she was moaning and crying out into his mouth and they were rolling around on the floor mindlessly, uncontrollably. . . .

"Do you think he heard us?" Pike asked later while they were dressing.

"He's sleeping soundly," she said confidently. "He didn't hear a thing."

She tucked in her shirt and went about trying to get her hair back in order.

"So, tell me about Sally."

"What about her?"

"You know," she said, not looking at him. "Are you friends?"

"I only just met her a few days ago, Sandy."

"As if that matters?" she asked, turning to smile at him. "I seem to remember we became friends fairly quickly after our first meeting."

"If that's the way you define the word 'friends,'" he said, "then no, we aren't friends."

"Yet."

"*Yet* doesn't come into it," he said. "I won't be seeing her again, except around this settlement over the next couple of days."

"And after that?"

"After that Skins and I will be on our way."

"And what about Sally? And Father Smets? And the others?"

"They'll be on their way, too."

"Without you?" she said. "I thought . . ."

"You thought what?"

"Never mind."

"Did somebody say I was going to guide them?" he asked.

"No, no one *said* it. I just assumed—"

"Well, don't assume," he said. "I just spent three

months all alone, Sandy, thinking about my life, and I'm a new man."

"Well, I'm just glad some of the old man was left for me," she said. "What do you mean, you're a new man?"

"I mean I'm staying out of other people's lives," he said. "Other people's problems are theirs, not mine. You're not going to catch me interfering in other people's affairs anymore."

"But you helped these people—"

"Helped," he said, "that's the key word. I helped them. They were alone, and had no supplies. I couldn't just leave them out there."

"So you brought them here."

"And here is where the help ends."

"All right," she said, "if you say so."

"Yes, I say so," he said. "How come nobody seems to believe me?"

"Who's nobody?"

"You, Skins... you both seem to think I'm just naturally going to keep on helping these people. Let me tell you what they have in mind. They have some crazy notion about finding the Flathead Indians, and observing them, and they'll probably want to educate them."

"What's wrong with that?"

"You can't educate Indians," he said. "At least, not like white men. They're not made that way."

"Father Smets said something about other missionaries?" she said.

"That's another thing," Pike said. "They're looking for missionaries who supposedly came up into these mountains a year ago, doing the same thing, looking for Indians. Let me tell you, they probably found Indians, and paid for it with their lives."

"Maybe," Sandy said slyly, "those missionaries didn't have a good enough guide."

"Oh, no," he said, "forget it. The last thing I'll do is

guide them out of guilt. I don't feel any guilt, thank you."

"I didn't say you did."

He fell silent and she smiled at him.

"Come back later?"

"We can't do this again, Sandy," he said. "Somebody could come in. Father Smets could wake up. We might have been—"

"Relax," she said. "I'll have someone watch him and we can go out back."

"Well," he said, "that would be different."

"Then you'll come back?"

"Sure."

"Good."

She walked to him and kissed him shortly.

"Am I back in one piece?" she asked.

"And a pretty piece it is."

"Thank you, sir."

He went to the door and opened it, then turned and asked, "Who are you going to get to watch him?"

"One of those missionary women," she said. "I'm sure they would want to sit with him anyway. Which one do you think I should ask?"

"What are you asking me for?" he asked. "You're the nurse, you decide."

TEN

From Sandy's, Pike went directly to the campsite he would be sharing with McConnell and saw to it that his gear was in order. It was dark, and McConnell was not around. Pike assumed that he had gone in search of some willing female companionship. Pike knew that McConnell liked Glory, but she was not the kind of girl who could be rushed. Besides which, he didn't really know if his friend had those kinds of designs on the young woman.

He knew that he had those kinds of designs on Sally—that is, he *did* before they came to Bonneville's Fort. He didn't really see how he could maintain that kind of a relationship with Sandy *and* Sally . . . and stay alive.

Pike was worn out, from the day's trip and the session with Sandy, so he decided to turn in early and get an early start on the next day.

Sometime during the night he heard McConnell come into camp and roll himself up in his blanket. His friend fell right to sleep, which confirmed his suspicions about where he had been. He laid awake for a little while, staring at the stars, thinking about Father Smets and Flathead Indians, and about Sally *and* Sandy. He finally rolled over on his side and, closing his eyes, willed himself to go to sleep.

In the morning Pike rose before McConnell and left his friend asleep. He walked into the settlement to get himself some breakfast. When he entered the saloon the bartender, Al, was behind the bar.

"Breakfast?" Al asked.

"Yeah."

"I got eggs," Al said.

"Sounds good," Pike said, "with whatever else you've got."

"Comin' up."

After a few minutes Al brought some eggs over to the table, together with some spuds and biscuits, and a pot of coffee.

"Heard we got us some missionaries in the settlement," he said to Pike.

"That's right."

"Gonna build us a church, are they?"

"I doubt it," Pike said. "I think they're out to civilize some Indians."

"Oh," Al said. "Well, too bad."

"What's too bad?" Pike asked as the man turned to walk away. "That they won't be building a church?"

"No," Al said, "that they're gonna go and get themselves killed."

"Who says they are?" Pike asked.

Al shrugged. "Ya can't civilize Indians, Pike, you know that."

Al walked away and Pike poured himself some coffee and chewed thoughtfully on his eggs. He wondered if McConnell had done anything yet about finding Father Smets, Sally, and the others a guide.

Pike was almost finished with his breakfast when Kenyon walked in. He saw Pike and walked over to his table.

"Have some breakfast, Kenyon?" Pike asked.

"Had mine hours ago," Kenyon said, "but I will have some coffee."

Al brought over another cup while Kenyon took a seat, and Pike poured it full for him.

"I talked to Skins yesterday," Kenyon said.

"About what?"

"He said those missionaries were looking for a guide," the *booshway* said. "Somebody who could take them to the Flathead Indians."

"That's right," Pike said. "You got somebody in mind for the job?"

"Just two men," Kenyon said. "One of them is Jim Bridger. He's married to a Flathead woman, you know."

Pike did know that, but he had forgotten.

"That's right. Is Bridger around?"

"Not around here," Kenyon said. "Fact is, I haven't seen Bridger in months, maybe a year. Maybe longer than I seen you."

"Who's the other man, then?"

"That's easy," Kenyon said, putting his cup down. "You."

"Oh no," Pike said, "I've already turned down the job, thank you."

"Why?"

"Because I've had enough of taking on other people's miseries," Pike said. "I've got plenty of my own to take care of."

"You helped them already, though," Kenyon said, frowning, "least, that's what I heard."

"I helped them once because I was there and there

was nobody else around to do it," Pike said. "That's not the case here."

"Sure it is," Kenyon said. "I don't know anybody else I'd recommend as a guide. Fact is, if they're gonna do what I heard, go looking for the Flathead Indians—"

"They are."

"They're gonna get themselves killed," Kenyon said, shaking his head, "if not by the Flatheads, then maybe the Crow or Blackfoot—or some animal. Seems to me if you ain't gonna guide them the least you could do is talk them out of it."

Pike didn't think he could, not after they had come all this way and gone through as much as they had. At least, he didn't think he could talk Father Smets or Sally out of it. The two priests would probably be glad to turn back. As for Glory, she'd probably just blindly follow Father Smets and Sally.

Maybe Kenyon had a point. Maybe the least he could do was try to talk them out of it. At least then he'd know that he had done his best to keep them alive.

"Think about it, Pike," Kenyon said, standing up.

"Wait a minute," Pike said, as Kenyon headed for the door.

"What?"

"Did you come in here just to tell me that?"

Kenyon looked around for a moment, then said, "Yeah, I guess I did."

After breakfast Pike walked over to the missionary campsite. As he had expected, Sally was already awake and toiling over the fire. Fathers Santini and O'Neil were still wrapped in their blankets. He assumed that Glory was in the tent.

As Pike approached the fire Sally looked up at him and almost smiled before catching herself.

"Good morning," Pike said.

"Good morning," she replied. "Coffee is ready. Would you like a cup?"

"Sure," Pike said, "thanks."

She handed him the cup and asked, "What brings you here this morning?"

"Oh," he said, looking around, "I just thought I'd come over and see how you all were doing."

"We spent a comfortable enough night, thank you."

"Where's Glory?"

"She went to check on Father."

He nodded, sipped his coffee, and continued to look around.

"You're here to try and talk us out of it, aren't you?" she asked.

"Out of what?"

"You know what," she said. "You want to talk us out of going looking for the Flathead Indians and the other missionaries."

"Sally," Pike said, "I just think it's too dangerous for you to honestly consider."

"It wouldn't be," she said, "if we had reliable guides."

"Like who?" he asked with a frown.

"Like you and Mr. McConnell."

"I already told you—"

"Then don't try to talk us out of it," she said, cutting him off, "just to soothe your own guilt."

"Soothe my guilt?" he said. "Guilt about what?"

"About letting us go to our deaths."

"Oh no," he said, shaking his head. "You've got the wrong man, Sally. I'm not going to feel guilty, because I have nothing to feel guilty about."

"If that was true," she shot back, "you wouldn't be here trying to talk us out of it."

"That's crazy," he said after a moment. "Just because I'm concerned for your welfare . . . and the welfare of

89

the others . . . doesn't mean I have any guilt."

"If you say so."

"It doesn't!"

"I believe you," she said, not looking at him.

"No you don't!"

"If you didn't feel some guilt," she said, "it wouldn't matter to you whether I did or not."

He gaped at her for a few moments. "You are the most stubborn, infuriating woman," he sputtered.

"Why don't you go and see your friend Sandy, then?" Sally said. "I suppose she's not stubborn at all."

"As a matter of fact," Pike said, "she's just as stubborn as you are."

"Are you trying to tell me that I have something in common with that . . . that . . . *mountain woman?*" she demanded.

Pike hesitated a moment. "More than you know."

"Well, I know one thing we do not have in common."

"And what's that?"

Still not looking at him she said, "Letting you in our bed."

Pike dumped the remnants of his coffee into the fire and put the cup down.

"You don't have a bed," he said, and walked away.

ELEVEN

Pike went to Sandy's then, not to see Sandy, but to talk to Father Smets. When he entered he saw the door to the other room open. Through it he could see Glory sitting next to Father Smets on the bed. Sandy was not around. Glory saw him and came out.

"Where's Sandy?" he asked.

"She had to go out," Glory said. "Someone is having a baby."

"How is he?" Pike asked.

"He's fine," she said.

"Is he awake?"

"Yes," she said, "and he was just asking me to go and find you."

"I'll go and talk to him."

She nodded. "I'll wait out here."

He walked past her into the other room. Father Smets turned his head and smiled when he saw Pike.

"I believe in 'Ask and it shall be given you,'" Father Smets said, "but that was fast. Hello, Pike."

Pike approached the bed.

"I was coming to see you anyway, Andy," Pike said.

"Oh? About what?"

"Probably the same thing you wanted to see me

about," Pike said.

"And what's that?"

"Being your guide."

"I see," Father Smets said. "Then you've decided to guide us?"

"No," Pike said, "that's not what I mean at all. I've come to try and talk you out of going."

"That would be a practice in futility, my friend," Father Smets said. "If that is why you have come, I advise you to save your breath."

"Andy . . . it's insane. How can you hope to civilize savages?"

"You believe the Indians are savages?"

"Of course."

"But you respect them," Father Smets said. "I can tell. How can a man as intelligent as you are respect people who are savages?"

"Because in their own way," Pike said, ignoring the compliment, "they are just as intelligent as we are."

"Intelligent people are not savages, Pike," Father Smets said. "It's a contradiction in terms. They are either one or the other."

"I don't agree."

"Then prove me wrong," Father Smets said. "Take me to the Flathead Indians and show me."

"Jesu—" Pike started, but stopped short when he realized who he was talking to. "You're just as stubborn as Sally."

"You have had this conversation with her?"

"Yes."

"And?"

"She's just as determined to get killed as you are," Pike said.

"And the others?"

"The others will probably just follow you wherever you go. You know that."

"Then your plea is falling on deaf ears, Pike."

Pike shook his head and said, "I guess you're right, Andy."

"I guess so," Father Smets said.

"So if you didn't want to talk to me about being your guide," Pike said, "what *was* it you wanted to talk about?"

"I wanted to ask you," Father Smets said, "if you would help me from this bed to the campsite. I must be with my people."

"Afraid they might bolt and run if you're not there?" Pike asked. "Especially two of them?"

"Actually," Father Smets said, "you're almost correct. I *am* concerned about Fathers Santini and O'Neil. They absolutely need my presence to reassure them."

"You're so right about that."

"Will you take me?"

"Let me talk to Sandy first," Pike said, "and I'll let you know."

"I warn you," Father Smets said, "if you don't help me, I will find someone who will."

Somehow, Pike didn't think Father Smets was just talking about getting out of bed.

Pike waited until Sandy returned. By that time Glory had left and Father Smets had fallen asleep.

Sandy walked in an hour after he had arrived, looking tired.

"Was the baby born?" he asked.

"Yes," she said. "It wasn't a long labor, but it was a hard one."

She moved close to him and kissed him hello. He could smell her perspiration, and it made him immediately hard.

93

"Just let me clean up," she said, "and check on Father Smets."

"I spoke to him this morning," he said, but left the rest of it until she returned.

When she came out of the back room she carefully closed the door. He noticed that her clothes were fresh, and that her hair was wet in places. He figured that she had gone out the back door to her shack and changed. He didn't believe that she had bathed, though, just washed up thoroughly. He could still smell her sweat, but it wasn't as pungent.

"Now, what were you saying about talking to him?" she asked.

"He wants me to take him to the camp so he can be with the others."

She thought a moment, then said, "Ordinarily, I would say no, but I think they'd take good care of him there, don't you?"

"Yes, I do."

"All right, then," she said. "I won't object, but wait until he wakes up on his own."

"All right."

"I'll send for you when he does."

"Fine."

"Are you going to do it?"

"Do what?"

"Guide him and the others."

"Why is everyone so interested in that?" he asked. "What do you know about it?"

"Well, he asked me if I knew someone who could take him where he wanted to go, and get him there safely. I told him no."

"Good."

"I told him I couldn't guarantee that someone could get him there safely," she went on, "but I did tell him that you were the one I thought he'd have the best chance with."

"Oh, fine," he said. "Thanks a lot."

"Did I tell him wrong, Pike?"

He stared at her a moment, then said, "No, Sandy, you didn't tell him wrong . . . exactly."

When Pike left Sandy he wasn't feeling angry. That surprised him. It seemed to him that everyone was after him. Even she, who probably didn't even like Sally—and the feeling was mutual—seemed to want Pike to guide the missionaries on their quest to find the Flathead Indians. Of course, there were other missionaries' lives at stake, but what were the chances that they were still alive after a year? And if he did let Father Smets, Sally, and the others go on alone—as they surely would if they didn't find a guide—would their deaths be his fault? Even if they weren't his fault, they would surely be on his conscience.

It was too bad, he thought, that Jim Bridger *wasn't* around. If he were, Pike wouldn't have to worry about any of this at all.

When Pike returned to his campsite McConnell was sitting up, pulling on his boots. They both wore boots when they were in a settlement, and moccasins when they were hunting and didn't want to make a lot of noise.

"I'm glad you're awake," Pike said to his friend.

"I'm not," McConnell said with a frown.

"We have to talk."

"I need coffee."

"I'll make some," Pike said, "and then we'll talk."

Pike started a fire and put the coffee pot on it. Soon the air was filled with the rich aroma, and even that seemed to perk McConnell's spirits. When they each had a cup warming their hands they sat down to talk.

"What's on your mind?" McConnell asked.

"Father Smets and the others."

"Tell me somethin' I *don't* know."

"Did you manage to find them a guide?"

McConnell sipped his coffee. "There are a couple of people available—nobody we know, and nobody who would do it for free like we would."

"We?" Pike asked. "You mean, you'd be willing to guide them?"

"Well," McConnell said, "I couldn't very well let you do it by yourself, could I?"

"What makes you think I'm going to do it?"

"Come on, Pike," McConnell said. "You're the only one who *doesn't* think you're gonna do it. In fact, you're the only one who doesn't *know* you're gonna do it."

"Oh, really?"

"That's right."

"And what makes you so sure—"

"Because I know you, my friend," Pike said. "You could no more let those people go looking for the Flathead Indians alone than I could, and that's what they'll do if they can't find a guide. You've been denying it all this time, which—if you ask me—is a tremendous waste of energy."

Pike opened his mouth to object, then closed it abruptly.

Sonofabitch.

"What makes you so damned smart?" he asked his friend.

McConnell smiled. "One of us has to be."

McConnell went with Pike to help Father Smets get from Sandy's to his campsite. They supported him between them, but did not carry him all the way. He wouldn't hear of it, insisting the entire time that he could walk.

When they reached the campsite they took him directly into the tent, where a cot had been set up for him. He seemed surprised at how well stocked the camp was, and also distressed.

"We can't possibly pay for all this," he said as they lowered him to the cot.

"Don't worry about that," Pike said. "It's all been loaned to you by a friend."

"A very generous friend," Father Smets said.

"Glory, would you ask Sally to come in here?" Pike asked.

Glory, who had followed them into the tent, nodded and went back out. Seconds later Sally entered.

"I want you to hear this too," Pike said to her. He turned to Father Smets. "Skins and I have talked it over, and we will guide you."

Father Smets and Sally exchanged unsurprised glances.

"We are very grateful," Father Smets said.

"We'll leave as soon as you're well enough," Pike said.

"I will be fine," Father Smets said sleepily, "very soon."

"Why don't you go outside and let him rest? I'll join you later," Sally said, putting her hands on Pike's arm.

Pike and McConnell went back outside.

"In a few days we will continue our journey," Father Smets said to Sally, "until we have reached a successful end."

"Yes, Father."

He closed his eyes and she squeezed his hand for a moment in both of hers, then continued to hold it until he was asleep.

TWELVE

Once he was committed to guiding the missionaries, Pike stopped worrying about the decision. The next morning he and McConnell outfitted themselves for a long haul with seven people, total. That was, of course, providing the other two priests accompanied them.

"You think they'll decide not to go along?" McConnell asked.

"I think they'll do whatever Father Smets tells them to do," Pike said. "I also know that *I'd* like it better if they weren't coming along. I mean, as far as I can see, they're totally useless."

"So?" McConnell said. "Talk to him about it. Tell him that we'd all be a lot better off without them."

"I'll do that," Pike said, "even though I don't think it will do any good."

"Good luck."

"What about Glory?" Pike asked.

"What about her?"

"Do you think you can get her to stay behind?"

"I don't think so," McConnell said, "but like you, I might as well give it a try. We'd move along a lot better if there were only four of us."

"And we'd attract less attention."

"Let's do it, then."

They split up, each going on a mission they knew was futile.

When Pike entered the missionary camp he saw Fathers Santini and O'Neil sitting by the fire. They weren't doing anything, they were just sitting, and wasn't that his whole point? They *never* seemed to be doing anything! Glory was there, too, but at least she was tending to the fire.

As he approached Father Smets' tent Sally came out. They both stopped when they saw each other.

"Change your mind?" Sally asked.

"No," he said. "I just want to talk to him about a few things."

"You won't change *his* mind," she warned him.

"I know him well enough by now to know that," Pike said. "Is he awake?"

"He's awake," she said. "Go on in."

She moved out of his way and Pike entered the tent.

"Ah, good morning, Pike," Father Smets said. Pike was surprised to see the man sitting up on the cot with his feet on the floor.

"Andy," Pike said, "you should be lying down."

"The sooner I sit," the old priest said, "the sooner I stand, and the sooner I stand, the sooner we can get started."

"We're not going anywhere until Sandy says you're okay to travel."

"Good," Father Smets said. "I trust her to make the right decision."

"That's kind of what I'd like to talk to you about," Pike said.

"Sandy?"

"No," Pike said, "making the right decision."

"About what?"

"Fathers Santini and O'Neil."

"Ah!" Father Smets said. "You have definite opinions about them, I know. You do not think that they should accompany us."

"It's not only them," Pike said. "I don't think Glory should go along either."

"Of course they are free to make their own decisions," Father Smets said.

"Come on," Pike said. "You know they'll do exactly what you tell them to do."

"And if I tell them to stay behind they will?"

"Yes."

"I can't do that," Father Smets said. "Not after they have come all this way."

"Andy," Pike said, "we'll travel faster without them, and we'll attract less attention."

The old man laughed. "I do not wish to attract less attention, Pike."

"Father," Pike said, "we're dealing with Indians here. They're liable to kill us as soon as they see us, without giving us a chance to talk."

"That's a chance we are willing to take," Father Smets said. "The Lord will protect us, Pike, and you and Skins as well."

"I like to be in control of my own destiny, Andy."

Father Smets nodded. "The Lord will take that into consideration, Pike."

"Those two out there," Pike said, "are useless, as far as I can see."

"They will be useful," Father Smets said, "when the time comes. They have done no more or less up to this point than I had expected of them."

"And Glory?"

"Glory will have a very special use when the time comes, Pike," Father Smets said. "I don't know if you have noticed it or not, but the child has a very special quality."

"I've noticed her, Andy," Pike said, "and she is not a child. Have you taken into consideration what the Indians might do to those two women?"

"They did not touch them the first time," Father Smets reminded him.

"You were lucky the first time."

Father Smets smiled and shook his head.

"The Lord was with us the first time, Pike," he said, "as he will be the next time, and the time after that . . . and after that."

When Pike left Father Smets' tent he was feeling frustrated. He stood for a moment right outside, rubbing his hand over his face. He noticed Fathers Santini and O'Neil watching him. Briefly, he considered trying to scare them into staying behind, but he decided against it.

He looked around and saw Sally, but he did not see Glory anywhere. Maybe McConnell was having better luck with her.

"Father needs me," Glory said to McConnell.

McConnell had come into camp while Pike was in the tent and asked Glory to take a walk with him.

"To do what?"

She shrugged. "To be with him."

"Glory, you don't know how dangerous this is going to be."

"It doesn't matter," she said. "As long as Father needs me, I will be with him."

"And if Father Smets told you to stay behind?"

"Then I would," she said, and then she added, "but

he wouldn't do that."

McConnell shook his head and hoped that Pike was having better luck with Father Smets.

Pike walked over to Sally, who was folding some clothing.

"Any luck?" she asked.

"With what?"

"With whatever you tried to talk Father out of."

"No."

"What *did* you try to talk him out of?" she asked curiously.

Briefly, he described to her the conversation he'd had with Father Smets.

"What do you think of those two?" he asked her when he was finished.

She looked over at the other two priests, and then back at Pike.

"Honestly?"

"Yeah," he said, "honestly."

"They're spineless," she said. "They're good priests, but I don't think they're very good missionaries."

"Well," he said, "I'm glad someone agrees with me about something."

"I don't agree with you about Glory, though," she told him.

"Why not?"

She stared at him a moment. "What did Father say about her?"

Pike frowned. "Uh, something about her being special."

"Yes," Sally said, "she is special, but do you know in what way he meant?"

"No."

"He means in a spiritual way," she said, "in a holy

way. Father Smets thinks that Glory is *very* holy."

"How . . . you mean . . . like a saint?"

"Well," Sally said, "she's not a saint *now*—"

"Wait a minute, wait a minute," Pike said, waving his hands, "she's just a kid." It didn't dawn on him that this was the opposite of what he had said to Father Smets about her.

"Many saints were just children, Pike."

"I don't see anything *saintly* about her."

"But you do see something special about her?"

"I guess so," he said. "I mean . . . she's *pretty* and all."

"Don't try to understand it, Pike," she said. "Just get us where we want to go, and then you and Skins can be rid of us."

"True," he said, "but when we do get rid of you, we want you all to be alive—and us too!"

THIRTEEN

On their fifth night in Bonneville's Fort Father Smets asked Sally to bring Glory to him. When she came back with the younger girl he said to her, "Leave us alone, please, Sally."

"Yes, Father."

When Sally was gone Father Smets said, "Come and sit beside me, child."

Glory obeyed, and sat on the cot next to the old man she revered and loved.

"We must move on," he said.

"I know, Father."

"I need your help."

She knew what he meant.

"I am afraid, Father."

"I know you are," Father Smets said, "but it must be done, or I would not ask."

"I—I know."

"Then touch me, child," he said, pointing to his wounded shoulder, "here . . ."

"What do you mean he can go?" Pike asked Sandy. "We only got here five days ago."

"I can't explain it, Pike," she said, "but I examined him this afternoon, and he seems strong enough to travel."

"That can't be."

"Well, it is."

They were in her bed, and had just finished doing their best to tire each other out. She was lying with her head on his shoulder, and he was rubbing one of her breasts, enjoying the way the nipple and the flesh around it felt.

"Even a strong man half his age wouldn't be strong enough to travel yet."

"Well," she said, "he *is* a holy man, let's not forget that."

"Are you implying that . . . that this is some kind of miracle?"

"I didn't say that," she replied quickly, "you did."

"Now wait . . . there are no miracles."

"Then you explain it."

"Is the wound still there?"

"Of course it's still there."

"Well, if it was a miracle wouldn't the wound be gone?" he asked. "I mean, isn't that the way miracles work?"

She laughed. "I don't know how miracles work. I've never seen one."

"Until today, right?"

"I still haven't called it that."

"That's what you *meant*."

"That's not what I *said*."

They laid in silence for a short time, Pike still rubbing her breast, and then he said, "All right, let's forget about miracles. If you say he's ready to travel, then we'll get started tomorrow."

"Then that only leaves us tonight," she said, sliding her hand down over his belly. She kept her hand moving downward, through his pubic hair, until she had his penis in her hand.

"Oh, not yet," Pike said, "I still need some time."

"We haven't got much time," she said, leaning over and licking his belly.

"Sandy—"

She moved her lips downward until she could touch the tip of his penis with her lips and tongue.

"I'm about to perform a little miracle of my own," she said, and took him fully into her mouth.

Pike rose very early the next morning and kissed Sandy goodbye. He had no way of knowing when—if ever—he would come back this way, and she understood that. Consequently, she had made it a night that he would remember.

He walked quickly to his camp and woke McConnell.

"Today's the day."

"Now?" McConnell said in disbelief.

"Now," Pike said.

"How could that be?" McConnell said. "It's only been a few—"

"I know how long it's been, Skins," Pike said, "but Sandy says Father Smets is strong enough to travel, and I told him I would go by what she said. You get the mules packed, and I'll go and wake the missionaries."

"Jesus Christ—" McConnell said, then stopped short and said, "Forget I said that."

When Pike reached the missionary camp he was greeted with a shock. They were all awake, and apparently ready to go. The tent had even been taken down. Sally gave him an amused look as he entered the camp.

"Are you ready?" she asked.

He looked at her in amazement. "Yeah, Skins and I are ready. How did you know?"

"Father Smets said we would be leaving today."

"How did *he* know?"

She shrugged. "I didn't ask him. I assumed he had spoken to you."

"No," Pike said, "he said nothing to me, and I didn't say anything to him."

"Well then," she said, "I suppose it was a lucky guess on his part."

"I doubt that," Pike said. "Get your people mounted, Sally, and meet us at the other end of the settlement."

"Father wanted me to tell you that we have *some* money and can pay for the horses."

"Fine," Pike said. "Kenyon will be glad to hear that. He thought he was donating them. We'll leave the money with him on the way out."

"It isn't very much," she warned him.

"That's okay," Pike said, "he wasn't expecting any. Does, uh, does he need any help getting mounted?"

"No," Sally said, "he'll be fine. We'll meet you right away."

"Fine," Pike said, "that's fine."

With a puzzled shake of his head, he left their camp.

When they met up at Pike's end of the settlement, Pike noticed that Father Smets was sitting up straight in the saddle, looking like anything but a man his age who was shot a week ago.

"I'm pleased to see you looking so well," Pike said to him.

"Thank you, Pike," the priest said. "The Lord has seen fit to give me back my strength earlier than anyone expected."

"I guess so," McConnell said, too low for anyone but

Pike to hear him.

Pike looked the others over. Sally sat her horse like she knew what she was doing. The other two priests looked the way they always looked, frightened and apprehensive. Glory looked remarkably relaxed and serene.

"Shall we get started?" Father Smets asked.

"Sure," Pike said.

Pike and McConnell had discussed the possibility of giving Fathers Santini and O'Neil some responsibility, such as leading the mules.

"I think I'd better hang onto the mules," McConnell said now.

"Sounds like a good idea to me," Pike agreed.

They decided to ride single file with Pike in the lead, followed by Father Smets, Sally, Glory, McConnell and the mules, and then the two younger priests bringing up the rear.

"If a mule gets away from me," McConnell said, just to see how they'd take it, "it'll be up to one of you to make sure it doesn't get too far."

The two men exchanged puzzled glances, and then Father Santini said to McConnell, "Which one of us?"

McConnell just shook his head. "Never mind."

FOURTEEN

In spite of the fact that the first day was uneventful, Pike was not encouraged. Their progress had been slow, and they had not covered as much ground as he would have liked. If they had been slowed by Father Smets he wouldn't have minded it as much, but it was the two younger, uninjured priests who were holding them back.

That night, after they had camped and both Sally and Glory had insisted that they should prepare dinner, Pike sat down next to Father Smets to eat.

"How are you feeling?" he asked the older man.

"If I said fine, you would not believe me."

"Andy," Pike said, "I'll believe anything you want to tell me."

"I am a little tired," Father Smets said, "and a little weak, but I will be fine in the morning."

"Good."

"You are not satisfied with our progress?"

Pike looked at Father Smets, wondering if the man could read minds as well.

"No, I'm not," Pike said. "We're an unwieldy group, Andy. Two women, two men who can't ride, and too many damned mules. If we run into a hunting party that wants to take us, we're going to be pretty hard-pressed to stop them—especially since McConnell and I are probably the only ones who will be shooting back."

"Sally can shoot."

"I know," Pike said, "I've given her a pistol, but *will* she shoot when the times comes?"

"That will be up to her."

"She'll look to you for approval."

"I will neither approve nor disapprove."

They ate in silence for a few moments before Pike spoke again.

"I'd like to travel at my pace tomorrow."

"We're in your hands," Father Smets said confidently.

"That means no slowing down for Father Santini and Father O'Neil."

Father Smets surprised Pike by giving a fatalistic shrug and saying, "They will have to try harder to keep up. They are not children, Pike."

"All right, then," Pike said.

"And the women?"

"I don't think those two will have any trouble keeping pace, Father," Pike said. "Sally can ride, and although I don't think Glory has spent a lot of time on a horse, she does seem to be doing very well."

"Animals can often sense when a person is special," Father Smets said.

There was that word again, used in reference to Glory—*special!*

"Will you be forcing Fathers Santini and O'Neil to take turns standing watch?"

"I don't mind forcing them to ride a little harder," Pike said, "but I don't think I want to put my life in their hands just yet."

"Then you and Mr. McConnell will be sharing the watch?" Father Smets asked.

"That's right."

"I could—"

"No," Pike said, "you couldn't, but thanks for the offer. The best thing you could do for all of us is get some rest."

"Yes," Father Smets said, "I suppose you're right. Good night, Pike."

"Good night, Andy."

Father Smets went to his blanket and wrapped himself up in it, moving not at all like a man who had recently been injured.

"More coffee?" Sally asked.

Pike looked up and saw her with the pot in her hand.

"Sure," he said, extending his cup.

She poured it full and then put it down on the fire and crossed her arms beneath her breasts.

"He's pretty amazing, isn't he?" she said.

"Oh, yeah," Pike said, "amazing is the word. I've never seen a man recover that quickly from a wound—especially not a man his age."

"I know," she said. "That's what I mean."

"Do you know how he did it?"

"Did what?"

"Recovered that quickly."

"The way he does everything, I guess."

"How is that?"

"With the help of God."

"You mean . . . like a miracle?"

"No, I don't mean that," she said.

"Have you ever seen a miracle, Sally?"

"I've seen some pretty miraculous things, Pike," she said. "But I don't think I've ever seen a miracle—not a real one."

113

"What do you mean, not a real one?"

"Well, Father Smets has heard some reports of miracles, but he's always been able to explain them away or expose them."

"So when you said he recovered with the help of God . . . ?"

"Oh, it's just something he says," she said. "He says God is always guiding his hand."

"Uh-huh."

"I've got to clean up," she said, "and then I'm going to turn in."

"Hmm? Oh, yeah, good idea. Tell the others to do the same. Skins and I will be standing watch."

"I could take a turn, if you like," she offered.

"No, that's okay," he said. "Get some rest. I'm going to push it harder tomorrow."

She grinned mischievously and said, "I'm sure Father Santini and Father O'Neil will be happy to hear that."

Pike nodded, barely hearing her. He was staring into his coffee, thinking about Father Smets' hand being guided by God.

"Who takes the first watch?"

Pike looked up and saw McConnell.

"I'll take it," Pike said. "I can't sleep anyway."

McConnell hunkered down by the fire and looked over in Father Smets' direction. The old man was lying with his back to them.

"How do you think he did it?" McConnell asked.

"Did what?"

"Recovered so quickly?"

"If you believe Sally," Pike said, "he did it with God's help."

"That's what Glory said." McConnell looked at Pike. "Do you think it was a—"

"Hold it right there," Pike said. "I don't want to hear that word anymore."

"What word?"

"You know what word."

"Oh," McConnell said, "that word."

"Why don't you turn in?" Pike said. "I'll wake you in four hours."

"Yeah, I guess I will," McConnell said. "See you later."

Pike waved. McConnell stood up and walked to where he had spread his blanket.

Sally came back to the fire. "There's still some coffee in the pot."

"That's fine."

"I could make some more."

"No," Pike said, "that's plenty. Just go to sleep, Sally."

"All right," she said. "Good night."

She walked over and laid down beside Glory, who was already asleep. Not far from them Fathers Santini and O'Neil had set their blankets down near each other. They were lying down, but Pike couldn't tell whether or not they were asleep yet.

When they were all down and quiet Pike poured himself another cup of coffee, picked up his Hawken, and moved away from the fire.

He found a suitable rock and sat down on it. Listening intently he heard . . . nothing. No, that wasn't right. He heard silence, that same eerie silence he had heard when they were walking to the settlement. He'd been in the Rockies a long time, and he had heard the various silences they had to offer, but he had never heard anything like this. But then, he'd never been in the company of someone "special" like Glory, or a holy man like Father Smets.

Had he?

Of course, this *total* silence would make standing watch a lot easier. He and Skins would be able to hear anyone approaching from far off, before they got too close. Still, even with that advantage, he would like to have been able to hear—oh, maybe just a bird in the night? Or some sort of insect?

This kind of silence was just too damn . . . *silent* for his comfort.

FIFTEEN

Father George Gentry stepped out of his tepee and looked around the camp. It looked the same as it had for the past year or so. Women working, children playing, men giving him the same looks. He knew that most of the braves in camp still wanted to kill him, after all this time. It was only the word of their leader, Strong Hand, that was keeping him and the others alive.

Of course, Strong Hand was also keeping him and the others from leaving.

Pike turned when he heard someone approaching from behind him. It was Sally, rubbing her arms against the cold night air.

"Can't sleep?"

"No," she said. "Can I sit?"

"Sure."

It reminded him a lot of that first night.

They sat in silence for a few minutes, and then Pike said, "What can you tell me about the others?"

"Others?"

"The other missionaries."

"Oh, them," she said. "I didn't know them."

"Did Father Smets?"

"Oh, yes," she said, "he certainly did. Father Gentry was a protégé of Father Smets'."

"A younger man?"

"Much. That was why Father Gentry went on the first mission."

"You've been with Father Smets how long?"

"Three years."

"And you didn't know Father Gentry?"

"He had moved to a different parish," she said. "When the diocese decided to send missionaries into the Rockies, they considered Father Gentry over Father Smets, for obvious reasons."

"The age difference."

"Right."

"Then why did the—why did they let Father Smets come this time?"

"They didn't," she said. "Father Smets organized this mission on his own."

"With his own money?"

She smiled. "Father Smets has no money of his own."

"Then whose money did he use?"

"Well, we took up collections, Glory and I, on the streets. Father Santini and Father O'Neil did the same thing in missions and churches."

"Ah," Pike said, "those two did something, huh?"

"Oh yes, they helped quite a bit."

"Still, that didn't get you enough money to outfit you, did it?"

"No," she said, "we still needed a sizable donation from a private source."

"A private source?"

"Yes," she said. "Me."

"You financed this . . ."

"Fiasco?" she said. "Yes. I had some money saved, and I was happy to give it to Father Smets."

"To do what?"

"Well, basically," she said, "he wants to find out what happened to Father Gentry and the others."

"How many others?"

"There were five people in the party altogether," she said. "Father Gentry, Father Callahan, Sister Margaret, Sister Florinda, and Brother David."

"Brother?" Pike asked. "Is that like a father?"

"More like a sister," she said. "Anyway, there were five of them."

"Were they all the same age?"

"They ranged from early twenties to Father Gentry, who was—is—forty-two."

"What can you tell me about the women—uh, the two sisters?"

She frowned. "What would you like to know?"

"Were they . . . attractive?"

"I knew—know—Sister Florinda," Sally said. "She's about twenty-five, and not *un*attractive. Uh, I, uh, don't know Sister Margaret, but I understand she's in her late thirties." She leaned back, studying him. "Why do you want to know this?"

"I just want to figure out what the Indians might have done with them," Pike said.

"Do, uh, the Indians . . . usually kill women who are not attractive?"

"Not always," Pike said. "Sometimes, if they're strongly built, they keep them alive, but they usually work them to death. Also, they keep women they think might be good childbearers."

Sally shuddered and rubbed her arms harder. This time it had nothing to do with the cold. She was thinking about what that kind of treatment could do to a nun, a woman who had given her virtue only to God.

"You better go to your blanket and try to get some sleep," Pike told her.

"I should have stayed there," she said, standing up. "You haven't told me anything that is going to help me sleep any easier."

"I'm sorry," he said. "I just thought I should know something about the people we're looking for. And that you should know something about how we might find them."

"As long as we find them alive," she said, "that will be enough. Good night, Pike."

He watched her walk back to her blanket, and wished that he could agree with her. She knew nothing about Indians, and had no idea that some things could be even worse than death.

Father Gentry walked through the village, acknowledging the greetings of the children. They loved him, knowing only that he taught them and made them feel better when they were sick. At their age they knew nothing of the hate their fathers felt for the white man. If Father Gentry had anything to say about it, they never would.

He missed the others very much. During his year here he had learned to speak the language. He did not get much chance to speak his own anymore. He would have liked to have a chance to talk with them, or even to know if they were all still alive.

Of course, he saw Sister Florinda, because she was in the same village as he, but he was not allowed to speak with her. She had been taken by one of the braves as his squaw, and had already given birth to one child and was pregnant with a second. He knew that in the beginning she felt great shame at having been . . . defiled, but he began to see a change in her after the birth of her first child. The fact of the matter was, even if he was allowed to talk with her, he didn't know that she would even reply.

At least she was still alive. He longed to know if the others were worse—or better—off.

Strong Hand watched Father Gentry from his tepee. The white medicine man was alive only because Strong Hand wanted it that way. The other braves, and also Dark Horse, the medicine man, wanted nothing more than to kill him, as they had killed the other one. In this man, however, Strong Hand had seen something special, something magical. Strong Hand's fortunes had soared since the appearance of Gentry, and as long as he kept the man alive he was convinced that he would continue to prosper.

Dark Horse also watched Gentry walk across the village. In direct contrast to Strong Hand, Dark Horse's fortunes had plummeted since the appearance of the white medicine man. If he could think of some way of killing Gentry without Strong Hand knowing he had done so, he would. At the moment he was not ready to challenge Strong Hand openly.

The day that he would was, however, growing nearer and nearer.

SIXTEEN

Right from the beginning Pike started pushing them harder, refusing to stop for as many rest periods as they had the day before. Fathers Santini and O'Neil fell farther and farther behind, but were still within view. To their credit—and it pained Pike to give them any credit at all—they did not complain.

Along around afternoon Sally rode her horse up alongside Pike and said, "They're pretty far behind, Pike." The tone of her voice was worried.

"I know."

"Don't you think we'd better slow down?"

"Look," he said, "the quicker we get to Flathead country, the less chance there is of our being attacked by the Crow, or Blackfoot, or Snake, or some other tribe. I'm not so convinced that the Flathead won't kill us, but I know we have a better chance with them than we do with any of the others. So, to answer your question again, no, I don't think we should slow down."

She fell silent, but continued to ride alongside him.

"We will be stopping for lunch, though," he added reluctantly.

"When?"

"As soon as we find a likely spot."

"Good."

That seemed to satisfy her, and she dropped back. Pike resisted the urge to turn and look behind him.

Twenty minutes later, he called their progress to a halt and announced lunch.

They already had a fire going by the time the two priests caught up. They said nothing, simply dismounted and tended to their horses.

"I think they're learning something," McConnell said to Pike.

"It's about time."

Sally and Glory made coffee, but Pike instructed them not to cook anything else.

"We'll eat the dried beef we brought," he told them, and they nodded and passed it out, followed by cups of coffee.

While they were eating, Father Smets asked his guides, "When will we reach the region indigenous to the Flathead Indians?"

McConnell frowned, but Pike understood.

"We're a few days away, Andy," Pike said. "We've still got to go a lot higher."

"And farther west," McConnell added.

"Let me ask you something, Andy," Pike said. "Just how realistic is your hope of finding Father Gentry and the others alive?"

If he was surprised that Pike knew about Father Gentry, he didn't show it.

"How realistic is your belief that you will still be alive tomorrow?" the old priest asked.

"I hate when they answer a question with a question," McConnell said to no one in particular.

"At the moment," Pike said, "that belief is a little

shaky—and it will become shakier still the farther we go on. How about yours?"

"I'm afraid it will take a little more than that to shake my beliefs, Pike," Father Smets said.

"Andy," Pike said, shaking his head, "it's been over a year, hasn't it?"

"Yes, indeed it has, but you see, Father Gentry is a very resourceful man, and he has been touched by the hand of God."

"Excuse me, Andy," Pike said, "but everyone on this trip seems to have been touched by the hand of God except for McConnell and me."

That brought a smile to the face of Father Smets. "Don't be so sure of that, my son."

As Father Smets walked away from them McConnell said, "So? Did he answer your question?"

"What do you think, Skins?" Pike said. "Some missionary from the East comes here and disappears. A year later, are we going to find him alive?"

"If he's anything like these people," McConnell said, "we just might."

Pike couldn't very well argue with that statement. These people had proven themselves stubborn and tenacious, and if Father Gentry had been taught by Father Smets, the man may very well have found a way to keep himself alive—other than just leaving his life in the hands of God. And what of the people who were with him? Could he convince savage Indians to keep them alive as well? If he were dealing with the Crow or the Snake, or some of the other warlike tribes, probably not. They took no pleasure in killing their enemies; rather, it was the only way they knew how to deal with them. As people who would like nothing more than to die at the hands of their enemies—if, indeed, they had to die—they would naturally assume the same was true on the other side. To kill your enemy was to honor him, unless you had no respect for him. In that case they would first humiliate you, and *then* kill you, but the way they would kill a dog, not a man.

Pike hoped that Father Gentry had learned well from Father Smets.

Pike allowed them half an hour to eat and rest and water the horses, and then he kicked the fire to death and told everyone to mount up.

When the others were all ready McConnell walked up next to Pike.

"There's that quiet again," he said. "I noticed it last night."

"So did I," Pike said, looking around. "It's just not natural, Skins."

"What *is,* with these people?" McConnell asked. "I don't mind tellin' you it's spookin' me a little."

"Well, I'm not ready to believe that it's magic—not yet, anyway."

"Magic, religion," McConnell said, "let me know when you've made up your mind, will you?"

"Yeah," Pike said sourly.

SEVENTEEN

Pike spotted the Indian, and was sure that the brave had been watching them for some time. He was up on higher ground, lying on his belly on a ledge. From this distance he couldn't tell what tribe the brave was from, but likewise, he knew the brave couldn't tell much about them. The Indian would wait until they were a lot closer before he made any kind of a move, and then only to return to his village with the information about them.

Pike stopped, and everyone stopped behind him. He turned in his saddle and exchanged a glance with McConnell. His friend handed Sally the lead of the mules and then he rode up alongside Pike. Pike dismounted and made a show of checking his horse's hoof. McConnell sat his horse, looking down at Pike. They were both very careful not to look up toward the lone brave.

"I saw him, too," McConnell said.

"Can you make out anything about him?" Pike asked.

"Not from this distance," McConnell said. "Whatever tribe he's from, he's probably just a lookout."

"Well, that means that we've been seen for sure,"

Pike said.

"The question is," McConnell said, "by who?"

"Whoever it is," Pike said, scraping some mud from the bottom of his horse's left forefoot, "we're going to have to wait for them to make their move."

"I hate to do that," McConnell said. "Makes me feel kind of helpless."

"I know what you mean," Pike said.

"What are we gonna tell the others?"

"Don't tell them anything," Pike said. He dropped the horse's hoof and looked up at McConnell. "They'll start turning their heads, looking around them, and he'll know we've seen him."

"Is everything all right?" Father Smets called out.

McConnell turned and said, "Fine, Father. We'll be movin' along in a minute."

McConnell looked back at Pike.

"We'd better keep movin'."

"Yeah," Pike said. He took a deep breath and said, "I wish we had more guns."

"The fact that we don't," McConnell pointed out, "might keep us alive."

"It might at that," Pike said, mounting up.

Eyes Like An Eagle studied the party as it stopped. With his excellent eyesight he was able to see them clearly now, while he was sure they could not have seen him.

He saw that the two women were young and attractive. One of them seemed frail, but the other looked strong, suitable for work and for childbearing.

Three of the men wore black clothes and white collars. Eyes Like An Eagle had seen men like that before. They were men who talked with the white man's God.

The other two men were white trappers and hunters. He did not know both of them, but as they got closer he recognized one of them. The very large white man was Pike, the one the Crow called He Whose Head Touches the Sky. Recognizing Pike, he was no longer certain that they could not have seen him, and he moved back from the ledge.

Uh-oh, Pike said to himself. The brave had abruptly moved away from the ledge. Okay, Pike told himself, so now maybe you think we've seen you. What's your next move going to be?

Of course, he could have asked himself the same question.

Eyes Like An Eagle left his position on the ledge and went to his horse. He would have to ride back to the village and tell his leader, the great warrior Crying Bear, that the great warrior of the whites, Pike, was riding through the Real People's land. Crying Bear would know what to do about it.

There was less than an hour before dark when Pike called out that they would camp.

While the others were making camp Pike went off to one side with McConnell.

"Did you see him leave?" Pike asked.

"I saw."

"By now he's told his leader we're here. We should get a visit sometime tomorrow, maybe in the morning."

"Well, that's what Father Smets wants, isn't it?" McConnell asked.

"I suppose so."

"Hey, those other two priests kept up pretty well today, didn't they?"

"They didn't have much choice, did they?"

Sally approached them, carrying a cup of coffee in each hand.

"Thanks," Pike said.

"Father Santini and Father O'Neil did better today, didn't they?"

"We were just talking about that," McConnell said. "I better see to the horses."

"What else were you talking about?" Sally asked.

"This and that."

"We were being watched today, weren't we?"

"Why do you say that? Did you see someone?"

"No, of course not," she said. "I *felt* that someone was watching us, but *you* saw him, you and Skins."

"What makes you say that?"

"That business with checking your horse's feet," she said. "What are you trying to protect me from, Pike? I'm already out here. We all are. What could be more frightening than that?"

"You're frightened?"

"Does that surprise you?"

"I haven't heard you admit it before."

"You never asked," she said. "Do you think that people who believe in God aren't afraid?"

"Well, judging from you and Father Smets, I was starting to think that, I guess."

"I can't speak for Father Smets," Sally said, "but I've been frightened ever since we left the church back home."

There was a moment of silence between them and then Pike said, "All right, yes, we were being watched today, by an Indian brave."

"From the Flathead tribe?"

"We couldn't tell," Pike said. "He was too far away

for us to see."

"What do you think will happen now?"

"I think we'll probably know that by tomorrow afternoon, maybe even in the morning."

"They'll come to get us?"

"At the least," he said, "they'll come to take a look at us, yes."

"We should be ready, then. I'll tell the others."

"Don't," he said, grabbing her arm as she started away.

"Why not?"

"There's nothing we *can* do to get ready," Pike said.

"Father Smets must know."

"Tell him, then," Pike said, "but not the others. I don't need them being extra jumpy tonight."

She hesitated a moment. "All right. I won't tell them."

"Good," Pike said.

"I'll get you your dinner," she said. "It should be ready by now."

He could smell the cooking bacon in the air—and so, probably, could anyone else within miles. It didn't much matter at this point, though. They'd been spotted. They might as well eat well tonight, because there was no telling what tomorrow was going to bring.

be,' or 'please God, *let* this be,' or something like that, sure. Who hasn't? That doesn't make me a religious man. I've also damned men in God's name."

"I understand," Father Smets said. "But I find your admittance that there is a God encouraging."

"Don't," Pike said. "Just because I use his name doesn't mean I believe in him."

"Why would you not believe in God?" Father Smets asked, genuinely puzzled. "Why would you *not* want to?"

Pike looked directly at Father Smets when he answered. "I've seen too many things, Father, that I don't think a God would let happen, if he truly existed."

"I expect you have," Father Smets said. "I hope, however, that I can do or say something that will change your mind."

"Only if you can change some of the things I've seen, Andy." Pike looked up at the morning sky. "You might as well start waking them up," he said.

They had breakfast, then broke camp, and mounted up.

"Let's just keep moving along like we don't know anything," Pike said to McConnell.

"You don't mind if I keep my rifle handy, do you?" McConnell said.

"No," Pike said, "in fact, I insist on it."

As McConnell went to fetch the pack mules, Sally rode up alongside Pike.

"Can I ride with you?" she asked.

Pike remembered what she had told him yesterday about being afraid.

"Sure, Sally."

Pike got them moving, not knowing just how far they'd get before they were stopped.

Pike heard them coming. It was then that he first noticed that the eerie silence was not with them anymore.

"Stop," Pike said, reining in his horse.

"What is it?" Sally asked.

"Horses," Pike said. "Unshod ponies, and a lot of them."

"I don't hear—wait, yes I do," she said. "I hear them."

"You still have that pistol I gave you?" Pike asked her.

"Y-yes," she said hesitantly.

"Make sure you don't touch it," he said, "understand? Don't touch it!"

"Yes," she said, feeling some relief, "I understand." She had been afraid that he was going to tell her to get ready to use it.

Pike turned and made eye contact with McConnell, who simply nodded. He noticed that Glory was riding alongside his friend. McConnell turned in his saddle and said something to Father Santini and Father O'Neil, both of whom suddenly looked ready to jump out of their skins.

"Let's go," Pike said to Sally, "slowly."

Before they could move, however, the Indians were upon them. They seemed to come from all directions, until they were surrounding them. Sally moved her horse closer to Pike's.

"Easy," Pike said to Sally.

Pike raised his hands in front of him, away from his rifle. He hoped that no one—namely the other two priests—would bolt.

A quick count told him that there were about twenty Indians around them, and they were definitely Blackfoot.

One of the braves rode directly up to Pike and studied him closely. Pike stared right back at the man, looking into his eyes. The brave leaned first one way and then the other, looking at the length of Pike's legs.

"You are He Whose Head Touches the Sky," the brave said to him.

"I am."

"Why do you pass through the lands of the Real People?" the Indian asked.

"We are on a mission," Pike said.

"What is this mission?"

"It is a mission to do great good," Pike said.

The brave's eyes went from Pike to Sally and then back again.

"This is your woman?"

"No."

"Why is she here?"

"Are you the leader of your people?"

The brave sat up straight on his horse.

"I am Iron Shield."

"You are not the leader."

Iron Shield did not reply. Clearly, he did not like being reminded of this fact.

"Who is your leader?" Pike asked.

Iron Shield hesitated, and then replied, "He is Crying Bear."

"I have heard of Crying Bear," Pike said. "He is a great leader. Take me to him and I will explain our mission to him."

Iron Shield glared at Pike for a few moments, then turned and spoke to his braves. Abruptly a brave rode close to Pike's horse and took his rifle, while another did the same to McConnell.

"Other weapons," Iron Shield said.

Pike removed his own Kentucky pistol from his belt and handed it to a brave along with his knife.

"Sally," he said, "give them your pistol."

She did not have it on her, so she had to dig it out of her things and hand it over.

"Does the other woman have a weapon?" Iron Shield asked.

"No," Pike said, "and the other men do not have weapons either."

Iron Shield made a motion with his arm and his braves checked Father Smets, Father Santini, and Father O'Neil for weapons. Pike would like to have turned and taken a look at how the priests were handling this, but he wanted to keep his eyes on Iron Shield.

When the braves were satisfied that the whites had been totally disarmed, Iron Shield once again looked at Pike.

"We will take you to Crying Bear."

NINETEEN

As they were led into the Blackfoot camp Pike was actually quite proud of his missionaries. They had all reacted very well to their capture by Indians. Of course, Fathers Santini and O'Neil were much too frightened to do much of anything, but still, Pike was satisfied with the way things were going. For one thing, he didn't feel that the Blackfoot were particularly anxious to kill them. Not right away, anyway.

As they rode into the village Pike looked around at the tepees, many of which were heavily painted. He knew that the painted lodge was very popular among the Blackfeet, especially the ones who were considered to be wealthy. Of course, wealth was relative. What a white man considered to be great wealth would be quite different from what an Indian thought.

"The paintings are beautiful," Sally said. "What do they mean?"

Pike explained why some lodges were painted more heavily than others, and still others not at all.

"Fascinating," Sally said.

She seemed, in fact, so fascinated that she appeared to have forgotten that she was afraid.

Pike and Sally were riding just behind Iron Shield,

who abruptly called their progress to a halt before an elaborately painted lodge. Iron Shield dismounted and entered the lodge. Moments later, he appeared with another man, who was a good twenty years or so older than Iron Shield, who appeared to be in his late twenties.

This was Crying Bear.

Crying Bear stared at the white people for a few moments, then said something to Iron Shield.

"Get down," Iron Shield said.

Pike was the first to dismount, followed by the others.

Their entrance into the camp was an event, and many women and children, as well as other braves, crowded around to see who they were, and what was to be done with them. Many of them were fascinated by Pike's height. There were many well-built braves in camp, but none had Pike's height, nor the breadth and depth of his shoulders and chest. Pike knew that many of the braves would find his size a challenge.

"You are the leader of these people?" Crying Bear asked Pike, in English.

"I am the guide," Pike said. "The white-haired man is the leader."

Crying Bear looked past Pike at Father Smets, then said something to Iron Shield, turned, and went into his lodge.

"You and the white-haired one will enter Crying Bear's lodge," Iron Shield said to Pike.

"What of the others?"

"They will be . . . cared for."

Pike turned and looked at Father Smets.

"Andy?"

Father Smets approached Pike and said, "I take it these are not the Flatheads?"

"No," Pike said, "these are the Blackfeet—although

they prefer to be called the 'Real People.'"

"And what do the Real People want of us?" the older man asked.

"That's what we're about to find out," Pike said. "Shall we?"

Father Smets nodded, ducked his head, and entered the lodge. Pike turned, looked at McConnell and then Sally, and followed. Iron Shield entered after him.

Inside, Crying Bear was already sitting, cross-legged, on the ground on the other side of a small fire. Behind him, to his right, an old squaw sat, working on a pair of moccasins. Pike knew that those moccasins would be very well made.

"Sit," Iron Shield said to them.

Pike and Father Smets sat on the ground, across the fire from Crying Bear, also cross-legged. Iron Shield remained standing, arms folded across his chest.

"Iron Shield has told me that you are on a mission," Crying Bear said. "Explain."

"We have come," Father Smets said, "my colleagues and I, to seek out the Flathead tribe."

"The Flatheads are old women," Crying Bear said. "Why do you seek them?"

"To gain knowledge of their ways, and to found a mission among them."

"I do not understand these words," Crying Bear said, and he looked at Pike for clarification.

"These people are missionaries," Pike said. "They wish to learn the ways of the Flathead, and then try to civilize them."

"Civilize?"

Pike sought an explanation that Crying Bear would understand.

"To make them like whites," he said, "to teach them of the white man's God."

"That is not entirely true—" Father Smets began,

but Crying Bear cut him off.

"The Flatheads are old women," he said again, "but that is still better than being like the whites." He looked directly at Father Smets. "You do not wish to do this to the Real People?"

"Oh, no," Father Smets said, glancing at Pike, "no, not to, uh, your people."

"That is good."

"We are, however, looking for some other people who, like ourselves, came to find the Flathead."

"Other people?"

"Other missionaries," Pike said. "They might have come this way many moons ago."

"I have spent much time trying to understand the white man," Crying Bear said. "I have learned his language."

"You speak it very well," Father Smets said, complimenting him.

"In white man's terms," the Blackfeet leader said, "how long ago did these other people come?"

"More than a year," Father Smets said.

"They are dead," Crying Bear said flatly.

"How can you know that—" Father Smets started, but the leader of the Blackfeet would not allow him to finish.

"If they came so long ago," he said, "then they are dead." He would brook no argument about the matter.

"What would you do with us now, Crying Bear?" Pike asked.

"You are He Whose Head Touches the Sky," Crying Bear said.

"I am."

"You are a great warrior among your people."

Pike said the only thing he felt was appropriate at the moment. "I am." He added, "as is Crying Bear a great warrior."

"There are those among my people who would question you," Crying Bear said, ignoring Pike's flattery. "Those who would challenge you."

"And I would accept their challenge happily," Pike said, lying outright. He knew, however, that this was the kind of talk Crying Bear would expect and understand.

"Very good," Crying Bear said, nodding. "We will see." He looked at Iron Shield and said something in his own language. Pike understood some of it.

"Iron Shield will have you taken to your lodges," Crying Bear said.

"We'll be staying?" Father Smets asked Crying Bear.

"Yes."

"For how long?"

Crying Bear stared at Father Smets. "Until I no longer wish it."

"But—"

"That is fine," Pike said, cutting Father Smets off. "We accept your hospitality."

Pike stood up, and Father Smets with him, and they followed Iron Shield outside.

"Hospitality?" Father Smets asked. "It sounded more like we were prisoners."

"We are," Pike said, "for as long as he wants us here. As far as anyone is concerned, though, let's just call it hospitality and let it go at that for now."

"Come," Iron Shield said.

The others in their party were nowhere to be seen, and Pike and Father Smets followed Iron Shield.

"What was all that business about you being a warrior?" Father Smets asked. "And where did you get that name, He Whose Head Touches the Sky?"

"The name came from the Crow," Pike said. "As for the other thing, it means that I just might have to fight our way out of here."

TWENTY

Pike and Father Smets were shown to an unpainted lodge. Inside, they found McConnell waiting for them.

"Where are the others?" Father Smets asked with concern.

"Sally and Glory were given a lodge together," McConnell said.

"And Father Santini and Father O'Neil?"

"I assume the same goes for them," McConnell said. "But I didn't see."

Father Smets looked at Pike gravely. "You don't think they've harmed them, do you?"

"No," Pike said. "They haven't had any reason to yet."

"Yet?"

"Well . . . they might decide later that they do have reason."

"Hopefully," Father Smets said, "that will not be the case. Tell me, what did you mean about having to fight our way out of here?"

"What's that?" McConnell said.

Pike explained to McConnell what went on with Crying Bear.

"You mean," Father Smets said, "you might have to

fight a man and kill him in order for us to be released?"

"Maybe more than one, Father," McConnell said. "Pike may just have to fight every brave who wants a chance at him."

"How many could there be?" Father Smets asked.

McConnell snorted. "A lot! Some of these young bucks would give their eyeteeth to be able to count coup over Pike."

"Well . . . certainly they would give you time to rest between opponents."

"No," McConnell said, "they'll make him fight them all one right after another until one of them kills him, or he defeats or kills all of them."

"But . . . but that's . . . *barbaric.*"

"Now you're beginning to understand," Pike said.

"No, no," Father Smets said, "we can't have this. I must talk to Crying Bear again."

Father Smets started to leave the tepee and both Pike and McConnell called out to him. He continued, stepping one foot out of the tepee, and stopping short when a Blackfoot brave blocked his path.

"Don't forget what we said about being guests or prisoners, Andy," Pike said.

"But I must talk to Crying Bear," Father Smets said again. "I must make him see how wrong this is."

"It's wrong to you, Father," McConnell said. "To these people it's only natural for a man to prove his courage by combat."

"But fighting and killing," Father Smets said, "it's against everything I believe in."

"But not everything that *they* believe in," Pike said. "You're going to have to understand this about these people, Andy."

"Maybe," Father Smets said uncertainly, "maybe the Flathead Indians will be different."

"Maybe," Pike said, although he didn't really believe

it. "But before we can deal with them we have to deal with these people."

"We have to talk to them."

Pike looked at McConnell, who just shrugged his shoulders helplessly.

Pike and McConnell moved to one side of the tepee while Father Smets continued to fret.

"You know, if you even kill one of their men we'll never get out of here alive," McConnell said.

"And if I don't kill at least one of them, they'll brand me a coward and kill us anyway."

"Damned if you do and damned if you don't," McConnell said. "So what do we do?"

"Let's try and figure out a way out of here," Pike said. "If we can't, then I'll just have to do the best I can when the time comes."

"It's times like this," McConnell said, "that I'm glad I'm not the living legend that you are."

"I'll remind you that you said that," Pike said, "next time we argue over whose turn it is to cook."

"I just hope we have the chance to have that argument," McConnell said.

Several hours later they were fed. An Indian squaw brought in three wooden bowls containing some kind of meat. Pike and McConnell instantly took theirs, sat down on the floor, and started eating it with their hands. Father Smets sat down next to them and stared at the meat.

"What is it?" he asked.

"Eat it, Father," Pike said. "We have to keep our strength up."

"Yes, I know," Father Smets said, "but I'd like to know what it is I'm eating."

Pike and McConnell exchanged a glance, and McConnell shrugged, leaving it up to Pike.

"Take a bite," Pike said.

Father Smets lifted a piece, sniffed it, then took a tentative bite.

"How is it?"

"It's not bad," Father Smets said, taking a larger bite. "But I'd still like to know—"

"We don't know exactly what it is, Father," Pike said, "but it tastes suspiciously like dog."

Father Smets stopped chewing abruptly, and Pike snapped, "Don't spit it out!"

The old priest stopped short of doing just that. He had his hand cupped beneath his chin to receive it, but obeyed Pike's command.

"Swallow it, Father."

The older man made a face, then swallowed with visible effort.

"Dog?" he said in a whisper.

"Possibly," McConnell said, chewing his with obvious vigor. They were all hungry.

"Likely," Pike said. "Go on, keep eating."

Father Smets looked from Pike to McConnell, as if seeking some sort of help.

"Just think of it as manna from heaven, Father," McConnell said with a smile.

Father Smets attempted to smile back, nodded, and took another small bite. Pike didn't care what size bites the priest took, as long as he ate it.

It had been dark an hour when Father Smets started fretting out loud again.

"I hope the girls are all right," he said.

"They should be," Pike said. Even if the braves *were* going to take the girls as squaws, Pike didn't think they'd had time to decide yet who would get them.

148

"And Fathers Santini and O'Neil," Father Smets said. "I'm sure they're frightened out of their wits."

"Maybe that will keep them from doing anything foolish," Pike said.

"Do you think we'll have an opportunity to speak with Crying Bear again?" he asked. "I'm sure I can get him to listen to reason."

"I'm just as sure you can't, Andy," Pike said. "I think we'd better just concentrate on getting some rest. There's no telling when they'll come for us."

There were already blankets in the lodge, so Pike grabbed one and passed it to Father Smets, then took one for himself. McConnell grabbed the third one and wrapped it around himself.

Pike and McConnell laid down, but Father Smets remained upright.

"Andy," Pike said gently, "get some rest. This will all sort itself out soon enough."

As Father Smets finally laid down, Pike knew that what he had said was true. It all would be sorted out, but he was almost certain it would not be in their favor.

TWENTY-ONE

In the morning Pike rose first, then McConnell.

"Let him sleep," Pike said to McConnell when he made a move toward Father Smets.

Pike moved to the lodge entrance and peered out. A brave standing just off to the right glared at him, but he just smiled and nodded at the man and drew his head back in.

McConnell was examining the rear of the lodge.

"If we had a knife we could cut through fairly easily," McConnell said.

"If we had a knife," Pike repeated. "You know, even if we got away they'd come after us. The Blackfeet don't like people thinking they can get away from them."

"Especially us," McConnell said, knowing that it was a matter of pride to the Blackfeet to outwit the white man.

"There's no way around it, Skins," Pike said. "If we're going to survive, I'm going to have to fight."

"The fightin' isn't the hard part," McConnell said. "It's winnin' without seemin' to win. You've got to go through every brave they throw at you without making them lose face."

"Won't be easy, will it?" Pike said. "They're going to

be trying to kill me and I'm going to be holding back. I could very easily get killed."

"Well," McConnell said, "if that does happen, maybe they'll let the rest of us go."

From the other side of the tepee Father Smets pushed himself up and said, "I don't find that the least bit funny."

"Out," the Indian brave said. He had simply stuck his head inside and uttered the single word.

Pike and McConnell exchanged a glance, and then got to their feet. They helped Father Smets to his, and then they all went outside. They saw the rest of their party—Sally, Glory, Fathers Santini and O'Neil—also standing outside, and joined them.

"Are you all right?" Pike asked Sally.

"Fine," she said. He could see that she was scared and trying to hold herself together.

"And the others?"

"Glory's been with me the whole time," Sally said. "She's . . . okay."

"How about you fellas?" Pike asked, turning to speak directly to Santini and O'Neil.

"What are they going to do with us?" Father Santini asked.

"I think that's what we're about to find out," Pike said.

He turned and surveyed the camp. It looked as if everyone had come out for the festivities. Counting squaws and children, they were outnumbered well over ten to one. There was an expanse of space between them, and in this space a circle had been drawn.

Off to one side, away from the others, stood ten braves.

"I think those are your volunteers," McConnell said

to Pike.

"Shit," Pike said.

"Hey," McConnell said, "there may be ten of them, but they're all smaller than you."

Pike gave McConnell a look that silenced him.

Iron Shield appeared from the crowd, followed by Crying Bear. Somehow, Pike felt it should have been the other way around.

They stopped about five feet from him, Iron Shield standing just slightly in front of Crying Bear.

Iron Shield raised his right arm, stiff and level as a lance, and pointed at the ten braves, all of whom were looking at Pike. It seemed to Pike that they looked particularly eager and hungry.

"They are your challengers," Iron Shield said.

"And if I defeat them?" Pike asked. He hesitated a split second and then added, *"All* of them?"

Iron Shield puffed out his chest and said, "If you defeat them, you will have to fight me."

"What's going on?" Sally asked.

"Crying Bear," Father Smets said, "we must talk about this—"

"Silence!" Iron Shield said. He was speaking to both of them, but still looking at Pike. "You will not defeat *me!"*

"But what if I do?"

This time it was Crying Bear who answered.

"Then you will go free."

"And my friends?"

"They will also go free."

"Crying Bear—" Father Smets said, but this time it was Pike's raised hand that silenced him.

"What about my friends *now?"* Pike asked.

"They may watch if they like."

"No," Pike said.

"Wait," Sally said, touching Pike's arm.

"I don't want them to watch."

"I don't understand, what's going on?" she said.

"I need time to prepare."

"You will have time," Iron Shield said, but did not say how much. He turned and walked away. This time, Crying Bear walked side by side with him.

"Pike," Sally said, "what's happening? They don't expect you to fight all those men, do they?"

"Well," Pike said, "not all at once."

"No," McConnell said, "just one right after the other."

"That's crazy!" Sally said. "Father—"

"Father Smets can't do anything," Pike said. He was sorry to have to tell her that, since she obviously felt that the old priest always had all the answers.

"But why are they doing this?"

"This is their way of proving whether or not we deserve to live."

"That's barbaric!"

"I suppose." Pike said. "Sally, I don't want you and Glory to watch."

"Why not?"

"It won't be pretty."

"Do you intend to kill all those men?" she asked.

"If I can."

"Do you expect to be able to do that?" she asked.

"Do I expect to be able to kill all of them?" he repeated. "No."

"Then what you don't want us to watch is you being killed."

"That's part true, yeah."

"Then we're staying."

"Why?"

"Because apparently what you're telling me is that if you die, we die," she said. "We want to stay."

"You haven't asked Glory—"

"She'll stay with me."

"Sally—"

"Pike," McConnell said, cutting him off, "they're coming back."

Pike turned and saw Iron Shield and Crying Bear approaching them.

"You have had time," Iron Shield said. "Prepare to meet your first challenge."

"What weapons will we be using?" Pike asked, removing his shirt.

"The weapon will be the brave's choice," Crying Bear said. "You will be given the same weapon."

Not only did he have to fight ten men, but he had to do it with their choice of weapons!

McConnell took Pike's shirt from him. "What's your plan?"

Pike grinned at his friend. "What plan?"

"Good luck," McConnell said.

"To all of us."

TWENTY-TWO

The first brave chose the tomahawk as his weapon. The weapon felt foreign in Pike's hand, but he was sufficiently superior in strength to the smaller man to ward off his blows until he could grab the brave's arm, break it, and strike a blow of his own. Even as they dragged off the still form of the brave, Pike did not know for sure if he had killed the man or not—although he suspected that he had.

"My God," Father Smets said, as Pike surrendered the weapon and rejoined his friends. The old priest was staring at the patch of blood on the ground that had come from the Indian brave's head, then turned and looked at Pike, who had nothing to say to the man.

"How do you feel?" McConnell asked Pike.

"Fine."

"That wasn't too bad," McConnell said.

"He was too small to make it a contest," Pike said. He was not even winded from the struggle, which pleased him. Still, he knew that wouldn't last. Even if they were all as small as the first brave—and they were not—fighting a succession of them would take its toll. Pike's mind was still working furiously, trying to figure a way out of the situation for all of them.

"Is he dead?" Sally asked.

Pike looked at her. "I don't know for sure, but I think so. I mean, I think I hit him hard enough to kill him."

She nodded, biting her lower lip. Pike looked at Glory, who seemed even more pale than usual. Fathers Santini and O'Neil looked green, and Santini had vomited on the ground. No one was cleaning it up, and both priests had moved away from it.

"To the circle," Iron Shield called out.

"Luck," McConnell said.

"Yeah..."

The second brave chose the knife as his weapon. Pike wished that he could have used his, but the one he was given was a good knife and he felt comfortable with it.

His challenger was slightly larger than the first one, but still significantly smaller than Pike. He was a good knife fighter, though, and it took Pike longer this time to come out the victor, and he did not do so without paying a small price.

As they dragged the brave away, there was no question in Pike's mind that he was dead. Pike had sustained an injury to his arm, and knew that he had no choice but to kill the man or be killed by him. Using his superior strength he overpowered the Indian and drove the knife into his belly to the hilt.

When he walked back to McConnell he was breathing harder than before, and bleeding from a shallow cut on his arm.

"You okay?"

"Fine," Pike said.

"You can't take that long to beat them, Pike," McConnell told him.

"The goddamned Indian wouldn't stand still," Pike

said. "I had to chase him down." Indeed, the Indian had nicked his arm while backing away, and Pike had to finally charge the man to finish him.

"There's eight more to go, and Iron Shield is waiting his turn," McConnell said. "You're going to have to beat them faster."

"Yeah," Pike said, taking a deep breath. "I know."

This time when he had killed the brave he had not only driven the blade in deep, but jerked it upward, effectively gutting the brave like a deer. He had decided to make a hard point, and the Blackfeet were looking at him differently now.

There was another puddle of vomit on the ground, but Pike couldn't tell which of the missionaries it had come from.

"This has to stop," Father Smets said, his voice shaking. Pike looked at the man and saw that he was paler even than when he had been laid up injured.

"There's only one way for this to stop, Father," McConnell said, "and that's for Pike to go right through all of those braves—or for one of them to kill him. If that happens, we're all dead."

"I—I thought you said you didn't expect to be able to kill them all?" Sally said.

"That was before he killed the first two so easily," McConnell said. He was caught up in what was happening and forgot who he was talking to. "Right now my money's on Pike."

"You would bet money—" Sally started, and then stopped herself. McConnell didn't have time to tell her that what he'd said was just a figure of speech.

"To the circle," Iron Shield said. When Pike turned, he saw that the Blackfoot warrior had come right up to them this time. They locked eyes and held them for what seemed like a long time.

"I'm coming." Pike said.

The third brave chose the lance as the weapon. Pike hefted his, testing its weight, and it felt alien in his hands. He'd held one before, but it would never have been his weapon of choice.

Of course, the brave who chose it was very good with it. He was not as light and fast as the other two had been. He was short, but stocky, with powerful legs and arms. He came at Pike, aiming to use that strength. Pike steeled himself, and the two came together with neither giving ground. The brave backed off quickly and brought his lance in low and hard. Pike tried to deflect it, but was only partially successful. The flint head of the spear caught him on the left hip. It went in and struck bone, and he backed away before the brave could twist it. He staggered and went down on one knee, losing strength in his left leg. He braced the back of the spear on the ground, and as the brave moved in for the kill he thrust it forward into the man's belly. The brave stopped short, his eyes widening, his nostrils flaring, and then his dead weight fell onto the spear, snapping it.

McConnell ran forward and helped Pike to his feet, helping him back to the others. Blood had already soaked into the entire right side of his pants. When they reached the others, Pike fell to one knee and braced one hand on the ground, his head hanging down.

"How bad?" McConnell asked.

"Bad enough," Pike said, gasping at the pain. "The sonofabitch knew what he was doing."

"To the circle!" Iron Shield called out.

"This is crazy," Sally said. She was leaning over Pike, her hands on his shoulders. "He's hurt!" she shouted at Iron Shield, who ignored her.

"They don't care about that," McConnell said, looking up at the Blackfeet. "They *smell* his blood now." He could see it in their faces. "They taste it."

"At least let me try to stop the bleed—" Sally started, but it was Pike who cut her off.

"No time," Pike said. He gasped again as he forced himself to his feet.

"Skins, he can't—" Sally said. "He's hurt too badly. He can't fight!"

Although McConnell agreed with her he said, "He's got to or we're all dead."

As Pike staggered back to the circle McConnell looked at Father Smets, who was praying silently, his lips moving, his eyes closed.

McConnell said a silent prayer of his own.

As Pike reached the circle Iron Shield said, "Prepare to die."

Pike turned his head slowly, looked at Iron Shield and said, "No, my friend . . . it's not a good day for it."

As Pike moved to the center of the circle to meet the next combatant the pain in his hip was almost unbearable. He could no longer even feel his right leg, and had to literally drag it behind him.

The brave he was facing looked across the circle at him with a smile. The man was so supremely confident that he could defeat the wounded white man that he chose bare hands as his weapon.

As the Indian moved across the circle at him, Pike made as if to move forward also, and pretended to fall. The brave, seeing this, rushed to finish him, but Pike swept the man's legs out from under him with *his* good leg. As the Indian fell, Pike grabbed him and, using his phenomenal strength, snapped his neck.

Once again McConnell rushed forward to help Pike up, but this time they did not even leave the circle.

"Leave me here, Skins," Pike said, gritting his teeth against the pain, "or I don't know if I'll be able to make it back."

"Maybe you should quit, Pike," McConnell said. "The rest of them are not gonna be that careless."

"If we're going to die anyway," Pike said, "I'd rather do it fighting."

"Maybe we should all die that way," McConnell said.

Iron Shield approached them. "Get out of the circle," he told McConnell.

McConnell straightened up and faced the brave.

"I think he's done enough, Iron Shield," he said. "What more do you want?"

"I will say when he has done enough," Iron Shield said. "He will keep fighting."

"Well, maybe we'll all do some fighting—" McConnell started, but with a wave of Iron Shield's hand McConnell was grabbed from behind by three braves, who pinned his arms behind him and dragged him out of the circle.

"Bring on some warriors, Iron Shield," Pike said, forcing himself to his feet. "All I've seen so far are a bunch of old squaws."

"You will regret those words, white man," Iron Shield said. "To the circle!"

The next warrior moved into the circle, armed with a lance. Since Pike had received his telling wound from a lance, the situation did not look good. He was handed his weapon and at least was able to prop himself straight up with it, but how was he going to fight if he couldn't move around?

The brave, who had chosen the lance *because* it was the weapon that had wounded Pike, moved in on him with the lance held in both hands, out in front of him like a staff. From the slow way he was moving, Pike knew he was going to pick his time. The thigh wound was streaming blood down his leg, and Pike began to feel weak and dizzy from the loss, but at least he could hardly feel the pain anymore.

"Come on, squaw," he said, goading the man, "come and get it."

Anger flared in the brave's eyes, but as he prepared to charge Pike a voice called out, "Stop!"

All eyes moved away from the circle, but as Pike turned to see who had spoken, he put his full weight on his wounded leg. The pain was so intense that he cried out in pain and fell to the ground.

He couldn't remember anything after that.

TWENTY-THREE

TWENTY-THREE

The first face Pike saw when he woke up was Sally's. It seemed to be floating above him; he felt as if he was seeing it through the heat waves that rise from the desert floor—but there was no desert in the mountains, and there were certainly no heat waves.

"What?" he said.

"How do you feel?"

He waited until her face came into proper focus before he answered.

"Terrible," he said. He tried to move and immediately felt worse. Pain rushed up from his thigh and filled his body and mind.

"Damn it!" he said. "What happened? Where are the others?"

"Now that you're awake," she said, "I'll get Skins. He can tell you."

It wasn't until she moved that he realized that his head had been in her lap. She lifted it, slid out from under him, and then set his head down gently on a blanket. He didn't bother turning his head to watch her leave. He heard someone enter, and then McConnell was towering above him.

"Sit down and tell me what the hell happened," Pike said.

McConnell did exactly that.

As Pike collapsed to the ground, McConnell turned his attention toward the voice. It was an Indian brave who had just ridden into the camp with a band of others. He sat his horse imperiously, and his voice commanded the attention of everyone in camp.

McConnell saw that Iron Shield was not happy to see the other brave. They were about the same age, contemporaries, but apparently also competitors.

Sally came up behind McConnell and pressed close to him.

"I know that man!" she said urgently.

"From where?"

"That's the Indian whose life Father saved. He kept Dolan from shooting him, remember?"

McConnell remembered Pike telling him about it.

"This," he said, "might work in our favor."

Then he went to check on Pike.

"I guess it did," Pike said.

"The brave—his name is Brave Wolf—kept us all from being killed by talking to Crying Bear. He and Iron Shield also had a shouting match."

"About what?"

"I think it's been going on for quite a while," McConnell said. "Since they were kids, probably."

"Is my leg still there?" Pike asked. "I can't feel it just now."

"It's there, old friend," McConnell said. "All bandaged, thanks to Sally."

"So what's our standing now?" Pike asked.

"Uh, that's still a little unclear," McConnell said.

"Where are the others?"

"Outside," McConnell said. "Father Smets wants to talk to you."

Pike made a face.

"Does he want to scold me for killing those braves?" he asked. "I don't think I can go through that with a straight face. Or maybe he wants me to—what is it?—confess?"

"I think he just wants to talk," McConnell said.

"All right, let him come in," Pike said. "But I might fall asleep on him. I'm feeling pretty groggy."

"I don't think he'll hold that against you," McConnell said, standing up. He started to leave, then turned and said, "Hey, old friend."

"What?"

"No matter what he says, you did good."

"Thanks."

McConnell left, and Father Smets entered a moment later. He walked to Pike and knelt at his side.

"Hello, Father."

"Are you all right?"

"I'll be fine," Pike said, "thanks to your friend."

"My friend?"

"Brave Wolf."

"Oh, yes," Father Smets said. "Pike . . ."

"Yes Father?"

"I, uh, want you to know that I do not condone what you did today—"

"Father—"

"—but I do respect why you did it," Father Smets went on, refusing to be interrupted.

"Well . . . thank you, Father."

"And I shall pray for your soul."

"Uh-huh," Pike said, "well, thanks, Father. I, uh, appreciate that."

Father Smets stood up and said, "You get some rest."

"Father," Pike said, "we really don't know what's going to happen after this, you know."

"Skins explained that to us," Father Smets said, "but the Lord has gotten us this far. He'll take us the rest of the way."

As Father Smets left the tepee Pike stared upward and muttered, "The Lord . . . yeah," and closed his eyes.

The next time he woke up he saw Glory's face. He knew that his head wasn't in her lap.

"Hi," he said. She wasn't looking at him and the sound of his voice made her jump.

"Sorry," he said, "I didn't mean to scare you."

"It's all right," she said timidly.

He looked around without moving his head.

"Where is everyone?"

"They're outside. Do you want me to go get them?" she asked. There was an eagerness in her tone, as if she wanted nothing more than to leave the tepee—or maybe she wanted to get away from him. What she had seen today—or was it yesterday?—was probably like nothing she had ever seen before.

"Sure," he said, giving her the opportunity.

Gratefully—it was written all over her face—she got to her feet and hurried from the tent. Pike really couldn't blame her for being frightened of him. Thinking back on what had happened, it was pretty frightening to him too. His blood had been racing hot during the battle, and he was willing to bet that his temperature had gone up. He *knew* that he had felt a special kind of satisfaction when he had broken that last brave's neck. There he was, barely able to stand, and he had still managed to defeat and kill a young, healthy warrior of the Blackfeet tribe.

He heard someone enter and saw Sally approach him, getting down on her knees next to him.

"How are you feeling?" she asked.

"Thirsty."

"Wait."

She got some water and brought it to him, and supported his head while he drank from a handmade wooden cup.

"Thanks," he said. "I guess I can't blame Glory for being scared of me, huh?"

"You realized that?"

"Oh yes," he said, "it was plain on her face, and the way she ran out of here."

"Glory has not reacted well to what happened," Sally said. "She is spending a lot of time talking to Father Smets."

"About me?"

"About you," Sally said, "and about her faith."

"Her *faith?*"

"Her faith has been shaken by the fact that God apparently let you kill four men by his design. Also, she has a hard time accepting the fact that you could kill like that and still be a good man."

Pike stared at her for a few moments, and for a moment he felt indignant—but only for a moment.

"I guess I can understand all of that," he said finally. "How do you feel?"

She took a moment to compose her thoughts before answering his question.

"I'm confused," she admitted after a long pause. "On

the one hand, I can't condone what you did, but on the other hand, I can admire what you *had* to do, and how you did it. I mean, you were *seriously* injured, and you were still able to kill another man. You killed *four* of them."

"It's not something to admire in a man, Sally."

"Perhaps not," she said, looking down at him. "But I see much *to* admire in you. For instance, your understanding of Glory's feelings. Not many men would be able to see that." She put her hand on his chest. "I think I have come to realize that you are a very special man, Jack Pike."

Pike didn't know how to react to that, so he said, "Tell me what's going on? What day is this?"

"You were wounded two days ago."

"Two days?"

She nodded.

"You've awakened once or twice a day."

"I only remember once."

"You had a fever for a while," she explained, "but it's gone down."

"I don't remember," he said, frowning. "Tell me what our status is now."

"It's changed."

"For the better, I hope."

"Officially, we are now guests of the tribe," she said. "Glory and I have our own tepee. Father Smets, O'Neil, and Santini are sharing one, and Skins has been sleeping in here with you."

"How about unofficially?"

"Skins says there are a lot of braves who would like to see you—the men, that is—dead, and would like to use Glory and me as . . . as squaws, I guess, or slaves. He says that Crying Bear is listening to Brave Wolf."

"How is Iron Shield taking that?"

"Not well," she said. "Skins says Iron Shield especially wants to kill you because you humiliated four of his braves and, by doing so, also him."

"I guess we'd better leave while we can," Pike said, attempting to sit up, "before Iron Shield is able to change Crying Bear's mind."

"I don't think that will happen." She put her hand against his chest to stop him and forced him to lie flat on his back again.

"Why not?"

"Iron Shield is not related to Crying Bear."

"And Brave Wolf is?"

She nodded.

"Brave Wolf is Crying Bear's son."

Twenty-Four

The wound was a deep one, and Pike was lucky to have avoided infection. It was five days before he could sit up, and another seven before he could get to his feet and remain standing without assistance. Even by then he was not ready to ride a horse.

For those twelve days Pike remained inside the tepee. The only news of what was going on outside came from McConnell and Glory. He saw Father Smets infrequently, Glory only once or twice, and he never saw Father Santini or Father O'Neil. One time, he woke and saw Iron Shield staring down at him. At least, he *thought* he saw him. It could have been a dream, but it seemed too vivid to him for that.

On the thirteenth day, McConnell entered the tepee. Behind him was an Indian. Pike knew it was Brave Wolf, because the man had been described to him.

Nevertheless, McConnell said, "Pike, this is Brave Wolf."

"Brave Wolf," Pike said, nodding his head from his seated position.

"I have come to see the white man who could kill four of my brothers," Brave Wolf said, "even when seriously injured."

"I had little choice, Brave Wolf—"

Brave Wolf held his hand up to stop Pike and said, "Brave Wolf understand that. He Whose Head Touches the Sky did what he had to do."

"I believe there are others in your camp who don't agree with that."

"You are wrong," Brave Wolf said. "All understand. There are many who do not like it, and still more who would like to kill you for it."

"Now we're talking about Iron Shield."

"Yes," Brave Wolf said. "Iron Shield most of all hates you. When you leave this place it would be wise to watch your back trail. I believe Iron Shield and some of the others will follow you and try to kill you."

"Can't you stop him?" Pike asked. "I ask not for myself, but for the others. McConnell and I can take care of ourselves, but the others . . ."

"They will have to take their chances with you and Mack-Connell," Brave Wolf said. "I can do very little with Iron Shield." Brave Wolf seemed to look inward and added, "It has been so since we were small children."

"If that is what we must do," Pike said, accepting it. To pursue the matter further would be taken as a sign of weakness.

Pike noticed Brave Wolf give McConnell a look, and his friend said, "Uh, Brave Wolf has another matter to take up with you. I'll wait outside."

Pike was puzzled, even more so by the amused look on his friend's face as he left.

"What can I do for you, Brave Wolf?"

"The woman."

Pike waited, then said, "Which woman?"

"The one called . . . Sally," the brave said. "I call her Bright Spirit."

Pike thought that over and decided that it was a

good name for Sally.

"What about her?"

"I have asked her to stay here with me when you and the others leave."

Pike was surprised, but managed not to show it.

"What about it?"

"She has told me that she is your woman."

Now Pike knew what was going on. Brave Wolf was asking him if he would give up Sally.

"Well, Brave Wolf," he said, "she is very valuable to me."

"Why?" Brave Wolf asked. "She cannot gut and clean a buffalo or a deer, she cannot make moccasins, she cannot cook—"

"She is valuable to me in other ways," Pike said. "In . . . spiritual ways."

For some reason Brave Wolf seemed to be able to understand that.

"I will give you three ponies for her."

"Brave Wolf—"

The brave held out five fingers and said, "Five good Indian ponies."

Pike hesitated. He knew that Sally had put the matter into his hands, and he wanted to play it right. He had to turn Brave Wolf down without insulting the man.

"Brave Wolf, your offer is very generous, and very tempting, but she has been with me for a long time and I am afraid that I cannot bear to part with her. However, I am honored by your offer."

Brave Wolf stared at him for a few moments, then grunted, turned, and left. Pike knew from the look on the man's face that he had played the situation correctly.

Just seconds after Brave Wolf had left, McConnell and Sally entered the tepee.

"What happened?" Sally asked anxiously.

Pike ignored her and looked at McConnell.

"Skins, I made a good deal."

"I hope you held out for five ponies," McConnell said, playing along.

"Seven," Pike said. "I got him up to seven, and you're to pick them out."

"I'll get right on it," McConnell said, and left the tepee.

"Wait a minute," Sally said, looking confused. "Let me understand this. You *traded* me for seven Indian ponies?"

"It's a high price," Pike said. "You should be honored."

"You *traded* me to that . . . that *savage?*"

"He wanted you very badly, Sally," Pike said, trying to hold back his laughter. "Or maybe I should call you Bright Spirit? That will be your name now."

"Bright Spirit?"

"Sure," Pike said, "I think it's a good choice—and think of what your kids could be called. Bright Wolf, there's a good one for a boy. Or Spirit Wolf, that'd be a nice, strong name for a girl."

"You . . . you . . . you . . ." she sputtered, and then he could hold it back no longer and broke out laughing.

"You . . . you . . ." she said, a different kind of sputtering now. She got down on her knees in front of him and reached for him. "I'll scratch your eyes out!"

Pike grabbed her wrists and held them, still laughing.

"Come on, Sally," he said finally, "it was a joke."

"Some joke!" she said. "If you weren't injured I'd—" She pulled one hand free and swung it at him. He leaned away from the blow, put weight on his hip and gasped at the pain the move caused.

"Oh!" she said, covering her mouth with her hands

and looking at him with wide eyes. "I'm sorry. Are you all right?"

"I'm fine," he said, caught between pain and laughter. "He really did want you, you know. But he only offered five ponies. You should have told me what you were doing."

"I know, I'm sorry," she said, "but it was all I could think to say when he asked me."

"Well, I'm flattered that you thought of me first."

"Well, I couldn't very well tell him I belonged to one of the fathers," she said, "and if I told him Skins, he might have wanted to fight him for me. You were the logical choice."

"Oh, I see," he said, "the logical choice."

"Yes," she said, grinning. "Still, even if you were healthy, I think I would have chosen you anyway."

She leaned forward, very easily and naturally, and kissed him, then rocked back on her heels and stared at him, shocked at her own action.

"I'm sorry—"

He stopped her by taking her by the shoulders, pulling her toward him and kissing her, this time longer. Her lips were rigid at first, and then they softened and relaxed beneath his.

"If you're suppose to belong to me," he said, "we should make it look right."

He could see that she was wearing nothing beneath her shirt. They were, after all, in an Indian camp in the mountains. He undid the top two buttons of her shirt, then pulled it down over her shoulders until her full breasts bobbed free. He leaned down and gently pulled on her nipples with his teeth and tongue, and then kissed her breasts as he held them in his hands.

"Oh . . ." she moaned. "Oh, it's been . . . so long . . . too long."

Suddenly, she stiffened and pulled away from him,

pulling her shirt back up to cover her breasts. Her eyes were fuzzy, and her lips swollen, and the rigid tips of her breasts pressed against the shirt, making little nubs in the fabric.

She swallowed hard and tried to get her breathing under control.

"Um, Father could walk in," she said, flustered.

"Sally, I'm sorry," Pike said. "I thought . . ."

"It's all right," she said, brushing her hair back and buttoning her shirt as she stood. "I have to go now. I'll—I'll bring you some food later."

"Sally," he said, but she rushed out without looking back. He was *sure* that that was what she had wanted—what they had *both* wanted—for a long time. Perhaps it had simply been so long since she'd been with a man that it frightened her, and she didn't know how to handle it. Still, given what she had done *before* becoming a missionary, her response was strange to him.

Maybe when she brought him his dinner later, they could talk about it. . . .

Twenty-Five

McConnell entered the tepee after Sally had left, and he had a puzzled look on his face.

"What did you do to *her?*"

Pike stared at him.

"I guess she doesn't have a sense of humor," McConnell said.

"She'll be fine," Pike said. "How did Brave Wolf look when he left?"

"Like his face was made out of stone," McConnell said. "I assume you told him he couldn't have your woman?"

"I told him."

"How many ponies did he really offer you?"

"Five."

"Good offer."

"How is everybody?" Pike asked.

"What do you mean?"

"Is everyone ready to leave?"

"You're not," McConnell said.

"Another couple of days," Pike said.

"Why rush it?" McConnell asked. "We got the chief and his son on our side."

"Let's not push our luck," Pike said. "What've the

missionaries been doing?"

"Father Smets has been talking to as many Indians who will listen," McConnell said. "Braves, squaws, kids, old people, anybody."

"Any converts?"

"Not a one."

Pike shook his head. "I don't want to wear out our welcome, Skins. Two, three days and I say we leave."

"All right," McConnell said. "It's gonna be your decision though. Whenever you feel you can sit a horse, we'll leave."

"I wish I could say *now*," Pike said, "but I'm still too stiff. I do think I could do with a walk, though."

"I'll go with you, to make sure you don't fall down," McConnell offered.

"I accept your offer."

Pike worked his way to his feet and then stepped outside. He squinted his eyes against the sun, but when he took a deep breath, drawing the mountain air deep into his lungs, he felt ten times better immediately.

They walked for about ten minutes, Pike aware of the looks he was getting—hard looks from most of the men, admiring looks from most of the squaws, and looks of awe from the children. The men's looks were for the most part filled with respect; though hatred bored through some.

Pike spotted Father Smets talking to a group of children, most of whom probably didn't even understand the language the priest was speaking. Pike suspected that the children were fascinated by the way Father Smets looked. The long black frock, the white hair, and the conviction in the man's voice drew their attention.

"Wait a second," Pike said to McConnell.

"What's the matter?"

"Jesus, I'm tired," Pike said, lowering himself onto a

rock. His hip was stiff, and he felt winded. He was aware for the first time of how much weight he had lost.

"Look at that old man," McConnell said, indicating Father Smets. McConnell voiced what Pike had just been thinking. "They don't even know what he's sayin' and they're listenin'."

"There's something about him, all right," Pike said. "What have the other priests been doing?"

"Hidin', mostly," McConnell said. "They're still scared out of their wits that they're gonna get killed. Also, I don't think they've recovered from what they saw you do the other day."

"Speaking of that," Pike said," how's Glory?"

"Well, I've kind of been workin' on Glory," McConnell said. "I'm tryin' to convince her that you're not the monster she thinks you are."

"Thanks."

"You don't seem real upset about that."

"Why should I be upset?" Pike asked. "First of all, it's her problem, not mine. Secondly, with the life that she's lived, I'm surprised she didn't faint."

"She did," McConnell said wryly, "right after you went down."

"Oh," Pike said. "Well, I can still understand why she wouldn't want to spend any time near me."

"Well, what it's gonna come down to is her either staying here, or leaving with us, so she's gonna have to get over it."

Pike stood up and took a deep breath.

"You ready to go back?" McConnell said.

"Yep, I'm ready."

They were halfway back to the tepee when McConnell said, "Uh-oh, here comes Iron Shield."

Pike saw the brave coming their way and did not slow his pace. He didn't want to show Iron Shield any weakness. The warrior seemed to see them for the first time, and headed straight for them.

"I am happy to see you walking around," Iron Shield said, stopping directly in front of Pike. Pike had to stop or try to walk over him.

"Sure you are," Pike said. "You'd hate for me to die before you could kill me."

Iron Shield surprised Pike by smiling.

"You are right," the warrior said. "I *am* going to kill you, and there is nothing Crying Bear or Brave Wolf can do about it."

"That's all right," Pike said. "I won't need their help."

"Prepare to die, dog," Iron Shield said.

"Not by your hand, Iron Shield."

The two matched stares for a few seconds, and then Iron Shield walked around Pike and went his way.

"That's a bad man," McConnell said.

"I know it," Pike said. He turned his head and watched Iron Shield walk away.

"Come on," McConnell said, "let's get you back to your tepee and get you something to eat. You're starting to look skinny."

Pike looked at his friend and said, "Skinny? You mean like you? Jesus, I should have traded Sally for those ponies. I'd eat one of them."

A half hour later Sally came into the tepee with food for him. Without looking at him she set the wooden bowl in front of him.

"Did you cook it?" he asked.

"No, the squaws did."

As she started to stand he reached out and grabbed her wrist.

"Sally—"

"Please let me go." She still wasn't looking at him.

"We have to talk."

"Pike—"

"Later," he said. "Come back later and talk to me. Okay?"

She didn't answer.

"Sally?"

"All right," she said. "All right, I'll come back."

He released her wrist and she left the tepee. He wasn't especially hungry, but he ate everything she brought. If he wanted to leave within three days, he was going to have to get his strength back, and fast.

Sally stopped just outside Pike's tepee, hugging her upper arms and staring up at the sky. She knew all along that Pike was awakening feelings in her she had not felt in a long time. Today, when he'd kissed her, when he'd *touched* her body, she couldn't believe how good it felt, and she had almost given herself up to it. Almost. She needed time to *think*.

Would giving herself to Pike be a sin? She knew that she should talk to Father Smets about it, but she dared not. She didn't want him to know that she was weakening. She would have to resolve this situation herself.

Pike was right. They had to talk about it.

Twenty-Six

It was two hours later when Sally returned, and Pike had almost dozed off.

"I'm sorry," she said. "I woke you."

"No," he said, "it's all right."

There was something different about her after only two hours. For one thing, she was looking right at him now, right into his eyes instead of avoiding his gaze.

She moved the empty bowl out of the way and sat down next to him.

"Are you ready to talk?" he asked.

"No," she said, removing her jacket and dropping it on the ground next to them.

"Then what—"

She put her arms around his neck and said, "I don't want to talk at all." She leaned forward and kissed him, her lips urgent, *demanding,* on his. Apparently, she had changed her mind completely in the last two hours.

"Sally . . ."

"Mmmm?"

"Are you sure?"

She unbuttoned his shirt and slid her hand inside, rubbing his chest.

"I'm very sure," she said, undoing the other buttons

with her free hand. "Very sure."

She peeled his shirt off, dropping it to the ground behind him, and then ran her hands over his chest. She leaned forward and ran her mouth over his neck, his shoulders, kissed his chest and his nipples, used her tongue to trace a path up to his mouth. When they kissed she slid her tongue into his mouth and cupped his head in her hands. He felt as if he were a cup that she was drinking deeply from.

She broke the kiss and sank back on her haunches in front of him. She unbuttoned her shirt and removed it, baring her full breasts. He reached for her, palming her breasts, feeling her nipples harden. She broke the contact briefly, to remove her boots and her pants, and when she was naked she came into his arms. He kissed her mouth, her neck, her shoulders, her breasts, tongued her nipples, then bit them. She was on her knees before him, leaning into the touch of his hands and his mouth when she felt him flinch.

"Your hip," she said.

"It's all right."

"No, it's not," she said. "Lie back, Pike."

"Sally—"

"Lie back," she insisted. He obeyed, lying down on his back. His feet were already bare so she removed his pants, being careful not to hurt him. When she saw his penis, huge and hard, she made an "oh" with her mouth.

"It's been a long time since I did this," she said, reaching for him, stroking him, "but I remember how. Just relax."

She began to kiss his chest again, then his belly, and then lower still until she was running her tongue up and down the length of him, wetting him thoroughly, and then she took him full into her mouth. As she rode him that way he moaned, but she could tell it was a moan of pleasure, not of pain.

She did things to him with her mouth that no woman had ever done. In the back of his mind he remembered that she had been a whore up until three years ago. He couldn't help but think that she must have been a good one.

Just when he thought he was going to explode she let him slide free of her mouth, and then straddled him. Rather than take her weight on her knees, though, she crouched over him, her feet on the ground on either side of him.

"I won't hurt you," she promised. She lifted her butt up and then shimmied down onto him until his penis was completely inside of her, and still she had not lowered her weight onto him. Still crouched, she moved up and down on him, sliding him in and out of her, doing all the work, bearing her own weight so as not to injure his hip.

He reached for her breasts as she rode him, squeezed them, pinched her nipples, and when her tempo increased he knew she was nearing her orgasm. She set her hands down on the ground on either side of his ribs and began to come up higher on him and then down faster, always making sure she stopped short of slamming her weight down onto him.

He felt his own explosion welling up inside of him and finally couldn't hold it back anymore. He went off inside of her like a geyser, and she closed her eyes and gave herself over to her own orgasm. She stayed on him until every ripple of pleasure had passed, until she felt him stop pulsing, and then lifted herself off of him. She still hovered above him though, using her tongue to outline his lips, and then driving it into his mouth in a deep, long, wet kiss.

* * *

She laid down next to him afterward, running her hand over his body over and over again.

"Sally," he said, "Skins could come in . . ."

"He won't," she said. "I told him to find someplace else to sleep tonight."

"You're bad . . ."

"No," she said, lifting her head and looking at him, "I'm not. I thought about this for a long time, Pike, after what happened earlier."

"I'm sorry about that."

"Don't be," she said. "We both knew this was going to happen. You awakened feelings in me that were long dead."

"I don't know if I should be proud of that or not," Pike said.

"Be proud," she said. "You know, when I was a whore I always enjoyed sex, it was the men I hated. I thought I hated all men until I met Father Smets. He never wanted to touch me. He took me in, and he taught me that there were other things besides sex."

"And I've ruined that now."

"No," she said, "thanks to you I know that sex can be good, as long as it's with the right person, and I can still go on working for the Lord."

"Unless Father Smets finds out."

She smiled and kissed him on the jaw.

"I'm sure Father Smets has an idea where I am," she said.

"And what we're doing?"

"Well," she said, grinning, "maybe he thinks I'm nursing you."

"Which you are."

"Yes," she said, "of course I am." She ran her hand over his chest and said, "I love your body."

"I wish I was able to be more active," he said apologetically.

"You will," she said, "after you've healed. Now I want you to get some rest. I'm going to stay here with you, if you have no objection."

"I have no objection."

"Good." She got up just long enough to get a blanket, which she brought back and placed over both of them. She pressed the length of her body to his—on his uninjured side—and the heat of her was intense.

They fell asleep that way.

Outside, Brave Wolf stood across from Pike's tepee. He had watched Sally go in, and now he knew that she was not going to come out.

He heard someone approaching him, but felt instinctively that he was in no danger. Finally, Iron Shield came out of the darkness and stood next to him.

"The white man has the woman you want," Iron Shield said into his ear. "If he dies, you can take her."

Brave Wolf said nothing. Ever since they were children, Iron Shield had been whispering in his ear, trying to get the chief's son to do something that he knew was wrong.

"I do not want her that way," he said finally. "I will welcome her if she comes to me willingly."

Iron Shield shook his head in dismay.

"I do not understand why you would want a white woman," he said.

Brave Wolf looked at his childhood friend. "We have never understood each other, Iron Shield. There is no reason to start now."

"Ah!" Iron Shield said. "If you would show the backbone that a chief's son should have—"

"Stop there, Iron Shield," Brave Wolf said. "You will not speak to me in that manner."

Iron Shield executed an exaggerated bow and said,

"I beg my future chief's pardon."

"Iron Shield . . ." Brave Wolf said wearily, but he did not finish. What was there he could say to Iron Shield that would make a difference? Since they were children, Iron Shield always had a mind of his own. He always did what he wanted, no matter what anyone else said.

"Go away, Iron Shield," he said finally.

"Yes," Iron Shield said, "I will go away and leave you here to moon over your white woman."

Iron Shield shook his head again, made a sound with his mouth to bring his point across further, and then melted away into the darkness.

Brave Wolf stayed where he was just a short while longer before he, too, faded into the darkness. Iron Shield's words still echoed in his ear.

"If he dies, you can take her . . ."

Twenty-Seven

Fifteen days after he was wounded Pike decided that it was time to leave. He had been walking for the past three days, and on that third day he found he was not so eager to go back to the tepee—except at night, when Sally came to him. Their sex was still gentle, because of his wound. He was looking forward to the time when he would not have to nurse his hip, and would be able to return to Sally what she had been giving him for the past three nights.

During his walks he had consistently spotted Father Smets talking to the children of the tribe. Frankly, he was surprised that their parents allowed it.

He waited, on that last day, for Father Smets to finish his preaching, and then walked over to the old priest as the children dispersed.

"Pike," Father Smets said, "you're looking well."

"I feel pretty good, thanks, Andy," Pike said. "We'll be pulling out in the morning."

"So soon?" Father Smets asked, looking disappointed. "Just when I think I'm finally getting through to these children."

"Andy," Pike said, "these children can't understand a word you're saying."

"The spirit understands, Pike."

"I'm sure it does, but don't forget you came up here to find the Flathead Indians, not the Blackfeet."

"I know, but—"

"And then there's your fellow missionaries. You're still looking for them, right?"

"Well, of course, but couldn't we just stay a little—" Pike did not allow the priest to launch another plea for more time.

"Tomorrow, Andy," Pike said. "We're leaving tomorrow. Okay?"

Father Smets looked as if he wanted to argue further, but he finally shrugged his shoulders and said, "Very well. You are in charge."

"That's right," Pike said, "I am. You might pass the word to those other two rabbits of yours. I haven't seen them in the past three days."

"Yes," Father Smets said. "Fathers Santini and O'Neil have been keeping out of sight. I will tell them."

"Good."

"What about Brave Wolf?"

"What about him?"

"Who is going to tell him we are leaving?" Father Smets asked. "He will be disappointed."

Pike, who had turned to walk away, now turned back to face the priest.

"Andy, let me explain something to you." He held out his hand, showing his thumb and forefinger with very little space between them. "We're still about this far from being killed, and we have to get out of here before we push our luck past the limit. As for Brave Wolf, he will be very happy when we leave, because then he can stop trying to keep Iron Shield and his followers from killing us."

"Really?" Father Smets said, looking surprised. "I hadn't thought of that."

"Well, I have," Pike said. "Round your people up, Andy, and if you want to tell Brave Wolf that we're leaving, that's up to you."

Pike turned and walked away from the priest. He had been very tempted, upon his recovery, to head back to a settlement and leave the missionaries to their own devices, except for two things. One was he knew they'd probably end up dead, and the other was that he had *almost* ended up dead himself, and because of that he wanted to see this through to the end.

Walking back toward his tepee he saw McConnell and Glory walking toward him. McConnell had Glory by the arm; if not for that, Pike thought she would surely run. They all stopped when their paths crossed.

"Skins, tomorrow is the day."

"We're leavin'?" McConnell said.

"Yes."

"Good," McConnell said, then frowned at Pike and said, "Can you ride?"

"I'll ride."

"Shouldn't you take a test ride first—"

"Don't worry about me," Pike said, "I'll ride."

"Okay."

"Have you seen Sally?"

"I saw her earlier," Glory said. She didn't look at Pike when she said it.

"Well, I'll find her and tell her," Pike said. He had discussed it with her last night, but had not made up his mind until this morning.

"Early start?" McConnell asked.

"As early as possible."

"We'll be ready," McConnell said. "I'll see to the animals."

"Let's see what animals they let us out of here with," Pike said.

"And what supplies," McConnell added. "If they

don't give us enough of our supplies back, we'll have to head the other way back to find a settlement to restock."

"I'm not turning around," Pike said. "We're going on. I'm going to find these people their Flathead Indians, and their fellow missionaries, and then they can do what they want."

"I'll talk to Father Smets about the supplies. He can talk to Brave Wolf."

"Fine. I'll see you later."

"Sure."

Pike walked away, aware that he had not made a favorable impression on Glory with his attitude, but he was suddenly very anxious to see the last of her, Fathers Santini and O'Neil, and Father Smets. Sally was another matter. He believed that if she wanted to leave the missionaries and go with him, he would take her, but he did not think that would happen.

As it turned out, Pike didn't tell Sally about his decision to leave until that night, when she came to his tepee.

"That's all right with me," she said, snuggling up to him. "The faster we get away from here, the better I'll like it."

He frowned. "Has someone been bothering you, Sally?"

"No . . ." The tone of her voice said that the answer was "Yes."

"Brave Wolf?"

"No, no," she said, "nothing like that. It's the women here, the way they look at me. It's as if they want to kill me, or they just want me to drop dead on my own. I've never felt anything like that, even when I . . . even *before*—"

"They may be jealous."

"Jealous?" she said, lifting her head and looking at him. "Of what?"

"Well, for one thing you're beautiful."

"Come on . . ."

"And they must have heard of Brave Wolf's interest in you. Does Brave Wolf have a squaw?"

"You mean is he married? No, I don't think so."

"Well then, that makes him a good catch, doesn't it? I mean, being the chief's son and all—and the fact that he's a fine figure of a man."

"I suppose all of that is true—and I guess that's why I want to leave."

"Well, we'll be getting an early start in the morning, so you'd better get some sleep."

"You, too," she said, putting her head on his shoulder and sliding her hand down over his belly like a snake.

"Sally . . ." Pike said warningly, but as her fingers closed over him he knew it was no use. They wouldn't be getting to sleep for a while.

In the morning, when Pike came out of his tepee, he saw McConnell leading a string of animals toward him. His and McConnell's horses were saddled and ready to go, the other horses—three Indian ponies—were packed up with more than enough supplies. Walking along with McConnell was Glory.

"Good mornin'," McConnell said, with a big smile on his face.

"Did you arrange for all this?" Pike asked him.

"Not me," McConnell said. "It was Father Smets. He talked to Brave Wolf yesterday, and Brave Wolf told him he could have anything he wanted."

"Have you checked the packs?"

McConnell nodded.

"We seem to have everything we'll need."

"Except for our three priests," Pike said.

"Two."

"What?"

McConnell nodded.

"Father Smets is leaving Father O'Neil here to continue the work he's started with the Blackfoot children."

Pike stared at his friend for a long moment and then said, "I don't believe it."

"Believe it," McConnell said.

"Believe what?" Sally asked, coming out of the tepee.

Pike relayed the information to Sally, who took it calmly.

"That doesn't surprise you?" Pike asked.

"No," she said. "If Father Smets asked me to stay, I'd have to do it. We're all servants of the Lord, Pike, and Father O'Neil knows what he has to do."

At that moment Father Smets appeared with Father Santini, both leading a saddled horse. Along with them was Father O'Neil. Father Santini had a look of relief on his face that he hadn't been the one told to stay, while Father O'Neil's expression was one of abject terror.

"He looks like he's gonna start cryin' any minute," McConnell said to Pike.

"That's not our problem," Pike said, "it's his. If he's fool enough to stay—"

"He has no choice," Sally said. "He has to stay in order to serve God."

"He can serve God without getting killed," Pike said to her.

Sally didn't say anything as she moved to meet Father Smets and speak to Father O'Neil. Glory moved away from McConnell and followed her.

"I guess you and Sally are getting along pretty well these days, huh?" McConnell asked.

"Speaking of getting along," Pike said, "where have you been sleeping the last few nights?"

McConnell smiled, looked at Glory, and then said, "Where do you think?"

Pike looked up as Father Smets approached them.

"We are ready to leave, Pike."

"Andy," Pike said, unable to help himself, "is it really necessary to leave Father O'Neil behind?"

"I have made so much progress with these children," Father Smets said, "that it would be a sin not to continue on. I *must* leave Father O'Neil behind."

"You're probably leaving him to his death," Pike said, "you know that, don't you?"

"Nonsense," Father Smets said. "Brave Wolf has assured me that Father O'Neil will be fine."

"Look at him," Pike said, looking past Father Smets at the younger priest. "He's terrified."

Father Smets did not look behind him, he simply repeated, "He will be fine."

Pike shook his head and said to all of them, "Let's get mounted up."

As they all climbed atop their horses Pike looked around them. There was not one Indian out this morning to watch them leave.

"Father Smets and Brave Wolf are so close," Pike said to McConnell, "why hasn't he come out to see his friend off?"

"Pike," McConnell said, "O'Neil's a grown man. If he doesn't want to stay he doesn't have to. There's nothing you can do."

Pike hadn't spoken two words to O'Neil in many days but now, before they rode out, he turned and said to the man, "Good luck."

He took one more look around, and even though he

couldn't see anyone watching them, he *felt* that someone was—and it didn't take much to figure out who.

Iron Shield watched as Pike—the vaunted "He Whose Head Touches the Sky"—rode out of the Blackfoot camp with the rest of his people, leaving one of the black-robed ones behind. Once they were out of camp, Iron Shield would be able to exact his revenge against Pike—and his first step toward that would be dealing with the man they left behind. After that, the Blackfoot warrior and his followers would go after Pike and the others. Pike would watch as, one by one, his people were killed. Then and only then would Iron Shield take Pike's life from him . . . slowly.

Also watching Pike and the missionary party's progress from camp was Brave Wolf. He didn't know what it was he liked about the white woman he called Bright Spirit. Perhaps it was because even though he knew she was frightened, she never showed it. Maybe it was because she would let nothing stop her from nursing Pike back to health. Or the way she withstood the stares and whispers of the squaws, both behind her back and right in front of her.

Whatever it was, he was not ready to let her go, not that easily.

Twenty-Eight

Pike actually reveled in being back on the trail again. It was a combination of his very real enjoyment of traveling on horseback in the mountains, and of the fact that they were away from the Blackfoot camp and alive when, several times, it had looked as if that would definitely not be the case.

He did tire fairly quickly, however, and his hip began to pain him so that he had to call their progress to a halt just several hours after leaving the Blackfoot camp.

"Are you all right? McConnell asked, riding up next to him.

"I just need a couple of minutes," Pike said, dismounting. He hated to admit it, but it would have been foolish to push himself and take a chance of them having to stop later for him, for a longer period of time.

McConnell dismounted and called out to the others to do the same. Pike heard him instruct Father Santini to watch their back trail.

Pike walked around a bit, trying to work the stiffness out of his hip and leg. He was standing still when McConnell came up alongside him.

"Did you feel anything funny this morning when we left the camp?" McConnell asked.

Pike nodded. "Like we were being watched."

"By Iron Shield, do you think?"

"Yeah," Pike said, "or Brave Wolf."

"Or both."

"Yeah."

McConnell looked back up the trail they had just come down. "I'd expect Iron Shield to come after us. He's not gonna forget what happened."

"I wouldn't expect him to forget," Pike said. He put his hands against the small of his back and leaned back, stretching. "He won't come after us this close to camp, though. He'll let us get a ways away."

"Think he's followin' us?"

"Why should he?" Pike asked. "He'll be able to find us when he wants us. He's probably glad we got all the packhorses we needed from Brave Wolf. It'll slow us down just enough for him to catch us whenever he wants."

Sally came over to them at that point and they stopped talking.

"Are we making camp?" she asked.

"No," Pike said. "We've got a long way to go before we make camp."

"Maybe you shouldn't push yourself so hard, Pike," she said.

"I'm not," Pike said. "That's the whole point of this stop, to give me just a little rest from the saddle. I'll be ready to go in a minute. Tell the others to stay ready, okay?"

"All right." She knew they were talking about something when she came up to them, and that they had stopped for her benefit. She had the good sense, though, not to ask what it was.

"I don't think Iron Shield will be following us," Pike said again, "but maybe you'd better ride drag and keep your eyes open."

"Right."

"Let Father Santini handle the pack animals. All he has to do is make sure he holds onto the lead rope. That shouldn't be too hard."

"I'll tie it to his wrist."

"Let's go, then."

"Listen," McConnell said, taking Pike's arm. "Stop anytime you feel the need."

Pike smiled at his friend. "I intend to," he said.

Pike stopped twice more before they finally camped for the night. On one of his rest stops he had told everyone to eat something because they wouldn't be stopping for lunch. When they finally camped McConnell and Father Santini gathered the makings of a fire, and Sally and Glory did the cooking. Both Pike and Father Smets sat down and rested. They were the two who needed it the most.

After they ate, Pike and McConnell set up the watch between them. Pike still wasn't ready to trust his life to Father Santini's eyes.

"You should go to sleep," Sally said to him. "I can take a turn on watch."

"I appreciate the offer, Sally," Pike said, "but there are things you just wouldn't be able to watch for. Besides, Skins is taking the first watch. Now get some sleep yourself.

She put her hand on his arm and he sensed that she would have liked to do more, but didn't dare in front of everyone. He put his hand over hers and smiled.

"Good night," she said.

Pike took the second watch because he felt that if he slept until first light he'd be too stiff to ride when he woke up. At least this way he'd be up hours before they left.

He wrapped himself in his blanket and laid down, but he couldn't fall asleep right away. His hip was hurting, and he was thinking about Iron Shield. It would probably have been better if he and the Indian brave had gotten it over with in the Blackfoot camp. Instead of making Pike go through those other braves, Iron Shield should have faced him first. But then, he thought, maybe that was the point. Maybe Iron Shield didn't want to face him. Maybe that was *why* he made him fight the others, hoping that one of *them* would kill him. Could it be that Iron Shield wasn't as confident as he appeared to be? Was he afraid of Pike?

That was the last thought Pike remembered. The next thing he knew he was being shaken awake by McConnell.

"Are you sure you're up to this?" McConnell asked.

McConnell had never had to shake Pike awake before. In the past he would only have had to call Pike's name.

"I'm all right," Pike said, unwrapping himself from his blanket. "Get some sleep."

He stood up and pain lanced through his hip. He flinched, but McConnell said nothing, which he appreciated.

"There's coffee on the fire," McConnell said. "I'll see you in a few hours."

Pike went to the fire and poured himself a cup of coffee, then took it with him when he went to sit a ways away. He was giving up the fire's warmth, but he was also removing the threat of being an easy target in the fire's light.

He held the coffee cup in one hand and rubbed his eyes with the other. He was surprised at how soundly he had slept after one day in the saddle. He would have thought he was in better physical shape than that, even after the injury. He realized that there were people in the mountain who considered him a legend. He wondered what they would think if they knew that he had given himself up so completely to sleep that McConnell had had to shake him awake. Certainly not the actions of a "legend."

Of course, he knew he was not a legend, he was just a man. Still, it bothered him that he had slept that soundly. It was undoubtedly due in part to his injury, he knew, and the loss of weight that followed. But he was starting to wonder if it wasn't also due to the fact that he was getting older.

Jesus, he thought, now I'm going to start worrying about getting older? So he wasn't as young as he used to be. So what? Who was? He was still in fine physical condition before the injury. He had felt as good as he had at any time in his life. All he needed to do was recover from the wound and regain the weight he had lost, and he would be back to normal.

He heard someone approaching and looked up to see Glory looking down at him. The light from the moon made her pale skin seem almost transluscent.

"Glory," he said, "can't you sleep?"

"No," she said, "something is bothering me."

"What is it?"

She noticed that his cup was empty.

"Would you like some more coffee?"

"Sure," he said, handing her the cup. She went to the fire, refilled the cup, and brought it back to him.

"Can I sit?"

"Of course."

Instead of sharing the rock he was sitting on, she sat on the ground at his feet.

"What's wrong?" he asked. When she didn't answer right away he said, "Maybe it's something you should talk to Father Smets about."

"No," she said, with an emphatic shake of her head.

"I must talk to you about it. It concerns you, and my treatment of you."

"Your treatment . . . I don't understand."

"Yes, you do," she said. "I have treated you very badly since . . . since you killed all those men. I would like to apologize, and explain it to you."

"Believe me, there's no need for you to apologize to me, Glory."

"Yes, there is," she said. "What you did you did for all of us, to keep us alive. I didn't understand that at the time. I was too . . . too shocked, I think."

"That's understandable."

"Sally and Mr. McConnell, they've made me realize the truth. If you hadn't done what you did, we all would have been dead long before Brave Wolf came back and saved us. That means that *you* saved us, and you almost died because of it." She got up on her knees in front of him, and then impulsively hugged him, her head against his chest. Surprised, he put one arm around her and patted her shoulder awkwardly. "You almost gave your life for us, the way Christ did. I want to thank you for that."

"Glory . . ."

"No, it's all right," she said, drawing back from him, "I know I've embarrassed you, but I wanted to apologize, and tell you how I feel."

"Well, I appreciate it, Glory, I really do. I'm glad you're not afraid of me anymore."

"Oh, but I am," she said sincerely. "You still terrify me."

He stared at her questioningly. "Why?"

"I've never known a man who could do what you did," she explained. "I mean, kill all those men, even with an injury that almost killed you, and then you survived. I—I've never—I'm sorry, Pike, but that still scares me . . . a little."

"Glory," he said, "you should get back to sleep. We're going to be starting early in the morning."

"All right," she said. "Good night, Pike."

"Good night."

Well, she had gone from terrified to "scared a little" in the space of a couple of seconds. At least that was something.

Wasn't it?

Twenty-Nine

Three days later they were approaching Flathead country. The morning of the fourth day Pike was feeling a lot better. He had taken the first watch that night, and when he woke he was not as stiff as he usually felt.

McConnell handed him a cup of coffee. "You're lookin' better."

"I'm feeling better too."

When Father Smets joined them, McConnell handed him a cup of coffee. The others were just getting up as well.

"Thank you," Father Smets said. "How soon do you anticipate we will encounter some Flathead Indians?"

"I wouldn't be surprised if it was sometime today," Pike said.

McConnell nodded his agreement and poured coffee for Sally, who had joined them.

"You're looking better," she said to Pike.

"I'm fine," Pike said.

"In what way will the Flathead Indians be different from the Blackfeet?" Father Smets asked.

"The biggest difference is that they're not as aggressive, not as warlike," McConnell said. "They may spot us, but they won't necessarily approach us. *We* may have to find *them*. And if they don't want to be found," he added, "it may be difficult."

Glory came over and sat next to McConnell, accepting a cup of coffee. Father Santini was the last to join them.

"Before we get started," Pike said, "I want to make sure we're clear on something."

"What is that?"

"When we meet up with some Flathead Indians—or any Indians—Skins or I are the only ones who will do any talking? Is that understood?"

"Yes," Father Smets said, and the others nodded their agreement.

"Second, I don't want anything that we do to be questioned—and I mean *nothing*. Understand?"

Father Smets hesitated this time before saying, "Yes, all right."

The others nodded.

"I think we learned our lesson last time," Sally said. "We all realize that you only did what you felt you had to do."

Of course, he thought, that wasn't saying that they thought he was *right*.

"Okay," Pike said. "Lastly, nobody says or does anything unless they're told to."

"How long do these rules last?" Father Smets asked.

"Father," McConnell said, "once we have successfully gotten you into the Flathead camp, the rest of your ... mission ... will be up to you."

"Will you be leaving then?" Father Smets said. "I mean, as soon as we find their camp, you'll be going on while we stay?"

Pike looked at Sally. "Not right away. As soon as we feel you're reasonably safe, *then* we'll be leaving to get on with our lives."

"Yes," Father Smets said. "I suppose this has been rather a drain on the lives of yourself and Mr. McConnell—especially on you, since you were seriously injured. I don't think I've expressed to you how sorry I am that you were seriously hurt."

"That's in the past, Andy," Pike said. "I'm looking at the future, and I want to make sure it is as smooth as possible."

"We will abide by your rules, Pike."

"Thank you," Pike said. "I suggest now that we break camp and get moving."

"We haven't had breakfast," Father Santini said. Those might have been the first words Pike had heard from Father Santini in weeks.

"So we'll travel lighter," Pike said.

Father Santini swallowed the rest of his coffee quickly, as if he thought someone would take it away from him, and then got up to help break camp.

As they saddled their horses, McConnell said to Pike, "I expected to hear from Iron Shield by now."

"He's probably making us wait," Pike said. "He wants us to wonder where and when he's going to hit."

"Maybe," McConnell said, "he's forgotten all about what happened, and we're waiting for nothin'."

They looked at each other, and then said together, "No."

Indeed, Iron Shield had not forgotten. He and a dozen of his followers had left the Blackfoot camp four days after Pike and the missionaries had, but they had already made up two days' time. They were traveling with one packhorse, but that did not slow them down.

Iron Shield's intention was to get ahead of Pike and his people, and leave something in the trail for them to find. He was not at all concerned with running into some Flathead Indians. He felt that any Blackfoot brave was worth ten Flatheads.

He knew that when Pike and the others found what he was going to leave for them, they would be gripped by fear, and that was when Iron Shield would make his final move.

When he was finished they would all be dead, with Pike the last—and slowest—to die.

Father George Gentry looked up as three braves rode into the Flathead camp. Father Gentry had been talking with three of the Flathead children, and now he watched as the braves dismounted and anxiously sought an audience with their chief, Strong Hand. Father Gentry watched as the medicine man, Dark Horse, intercepted them and listened to what they had to say.

The only thing that could make a Flathead brave that anxious was the approach of someone to their land—either members of another tribe, like the Blackfeet or the Crow—*or* the approach of white men.

In the year that Father Gentry had lived among the Flathead, he had seen very few white men.

He was interested in finding out what had happened, so he patted the children on their heads, and went to see if he could do so.

Dark Horse was dismissing the braves as Father Gentry approached.

"What is happening, Dark Horse?"

Dark Horse turned and cast a dark scowl toward the priest.

"It is not your concern," the medicine man said.

Father Gentry frowned, but there was nothing hostile in his expression. He was constantly puzzled as to why Dark Horse hated him. He certainly had never had any intention of replacing the man, and yet Dark Horse seemed to feel that they were competitors.

"If you do not tell me," Father Gentry said, "I will simply have to ask Strong Hand, after you tell *him.*"

Dark Horse glared at the priest. "Red Hawk has seen white men and women approaching."

"Men *and* women?" Father Gentry asked, surprised. It had been even longer since he had seen a white woman.

"Who are they?" he asked.

"I do not know," Dark Horse said, "but Red Hawk said there were two black robes with them."

"Black robes?"

That was what the Flathead Indians called Father Gentry, because of the black robe he wore. Although his was worn and had been mended many times by the tribe's squaws, he still wore it. If there were others approaching, then who were they?

"I must talk to Strong Hand," Dark Horse said, and walked away from the priest. Father Gentry hardly noticed. He was thinking about a man he had not seen for over a year.

Could one of the approaching priests be Father Adrian Smets?

Dark Horse entered Strong Hand's tepee and gave him the information. He did not mention Red Hawk's name, but simply said that a brave had seen some whites approaching. Dark Horse did not see any reason to give Red Hawk credit for the siting if he didn't have to.

"Two black robes?" Strong Hand asked.

"Yes, my chief," Dark Horse said. "You know how much trouble one black robe has brought us."

"Dark Horse," the Flathead leader said, "you know

that we do not agree on that matter."

"Still," Dark Horse said, "I do not think we need two more black robes here."

"That may be," Strong Hand said, "but it is possible they will not find us."

"It is possible," Dark Horse said, and then he told Strong Hand something he hadn't told Father Gentry. "They are being led by He Whose Head Touches the Sky."

"Pike," Strong Hand said. He had never met the white man, but he knew of the legend. "He is a great hunter, and a great warrior."

"Yes," said Dark Horse, "but is he hunting us?"

"That is something we will have to find out," Strong Hand said. "Send out a party to bring them here."

"I have a suggestion, my chief."

Strong Hand knew what Dark Horse's suggestion would be, but he said, "What is it?" anyway.

"I agree we should send out a party to meet them, but I think we should kill them."

"No," Strong Hand said.

"But—"

"We are not the Blackfeet, or the Crow," Strong Hand said. "We are better than they are. We do not kill without good reason."

It was precisely this attitude that Dark Horse blamed Father Gentry for.

"The warrior Pike is not to be trifled with, my chief. We should kill him when we have the chance."

"No," Strong Hand said again. "Send out a party to bring them here."

"As you wish, my chief."

Before Dark Horse could leave the tepee, though, Strong Hand said, "And send the black robe with them."

Dark Horse stopped short and turned to look at

Strong Hand. The two men matched stares for a few moments, and it was the medicine man who shifted his gaze.

"As you wish."

The day would come, he thought, when he was *not* the one who looked away.

Outside, Dark Horse found Father Gentry once again among the children.

"We are sending a party to meet the approaching whites," he told the priest. "Strong Hand wishes you to accompany them."

Father Gentry could tell that Dark Horse did not like the idea. As if the medicine man needed another reason to hate him . . .

"You will leave with Red Hawk and the others," Dark Horse said, as if the order was his.

"Now?"

"Yes. I will have a pony brought for you."

In deference to Dark Horse, Father Gentry said, "As you wish, my friend," even though he knew that Dark Horse did *not* wish, and certainly did *not* consider himself Gentry's friend.

As Dark Horse stalked off, Father Gentry felt his heartbeat quickening. He was excited at the prospect of seeing and talking with other white people, but the possibility that one of them might be his mentor, Father Smets, made him anxious as well.

Thirty

"We've been spotted," Pike said to McConnell.

"I know."

"What's wrong?" Father Smets asked, riding up alongside of them.

Pike told him.

"By who? The Flathead Indians?"

Pike looked at McConnell, who nodded his agreement that Father Smets should be told.

"Andy, it could be the Flathead, but it could also be Iron Shield."

"Do you still think he will come after us?" Father Smets asked, surprised. "I mean, I thought after all this time—"

"Men like Iron Shield have long memories, Father," McConnell said, "white or Indian."

"What do we do, then?"

"We continue on," Pike said. "Let's close it up, though, and ride closer together. Skins, keep riding drag but take the pack animals from Father Santini. If anything happens, cut them loose."

"Right."

"Have Glory ride next to you," Pike said, "and tell Sally to ride up here near me. Andy, you ride with

Father Santini, and keep him from doing anything stupid. He's your responsibility."

"He will be fine."

"I'm sure," Pike said, even though he wasn't sure at all.

They set up in their new formation and continued riding on that way until Pike spotted something up ahead in the trail.

"Stop," he said to Sally.

"What is it?"

Before answering, Pike made sure that everyone behind him had come to a halt.

"There's something up ahead," he said to Sally, "in the trail."

She peered ahead and said, "I see . . . but what is it?"

"I don't know," Pike said, even though he had a very good idea about what it was. "Stay here while I take a look."

McConnell rode up on them and didn't need to be told anything. He saw what was up ahead, and made the same assumption that Pike had. He remained next to Sally, with Glory just behind him, while Pike rode on ahead to take a look.

Pike rode slowly and carefully mindful of a possible trap. As he approached the object in their path he knew instinctively that he was right about what it was. He dismounted and walked to it, and saw that it was covered with a blanket. He took a deep breath and removed it just far enough to see the face. He found himself looking at the body of Father O'Neil. The man had been tortured, and his eyelids had been cut off. He had been dead for days. Instead of bringing him here alive and then killing him, they had killed him and then carried his body here.

Pike knew that other atrocities had undoubtedly been committed against the priest while he was alive, but decided that he didn't need to see them. He covered the body again, then stood up and stared straight ahead, breathing deeply. He felt an anger welling up inside of him, and wasn't quite sure who it was directed at—himself, Iron Shield, or Father Smets. Finally he looked back at the others and waved for McConnell to join him.

"What is it?" McConnell asked as he reached Pike and the body.

"It's Father O'Neil, Skins."

"Oh, Jesus," McConnell said. He got down and looked at the body himself. "They killed him and carried his body all this way?"

Pike nodded.

"Iron Shield is playing games with us."

"What do we tell the others?"

"What do we tell them?" Pike asked angrily. "We tell them the truth. In fact, we make Father Smets come and take a look himself." Now he felt that the anger was more toward Father Smets than anyone. Iron Shield may have *made* this terrible thing happen, but Father Smets had *let* it happen.

"Pike," McConnell said, "I don't think—"

"No, Skins!" Pike said, his anger growing. "I warned him. I told him he was leaving this man behind to be killed. I want him to see what they did to him. I want him to see what his God let happen to this man, who was supposed to be serving him."

"Pike—"

"Go and get him, Skins," Pike said, "and make sure the women stay behind. There's no need for them to see this, but I *want him* to see it."

McConnell hesitated, then decided that arguing with his friend would do no good. He also decided that Pike was right. Father Smets should see what had been done to Father O'Neil. Maybe from now on the man would listen to what they told him.

When he reached the others Sally said, "What's wrong? What is it?"

"Father Smets," he said, ignoring her, "Pike would like you to join him."

"Why? What is it?"

"Please, Father."

Father Smets gave McConnell a puzzled look, and then rode on ahead.

"What is it, Skins?" Glory asked.

He told them, and they wept . . .

Iron Shield watched as the white haired black robe rode to join Pike. He watched with a tight smile on his face as the black robe removed the blanket and looked down at the other black robe.

He could imagine the cold terror that closed around the black robe's heart when he saw the face of his friend, and he laughed aloud.

Father Smets stared down at the body of Father O'Neil for a long time, and then looked up at Pike, who was shocked at the serene look that was on the man's face.

"This will not shake my faith," Father Smets said to Pike.

"My God, man," Pike said, "that man was your friend. I *told* you that you were leaving him to die, but you wouldn't believe me."

"I thought—"

"No, Father," Pike said, "you *didn't* think. That's the problem."

As Pike walked away he heard Father Smets begin to pray.

When he reached the others, he saw that Sally and Glory were crying, and Father Santini had a shocked look on his face. McConnell merely appeared solemn.

"We'll have to bury him before we move on," Pike said, and McConnell nodded.

"I will help," Father Santini said.

"There's no need for you to see him, Father—" Pike started, but the young priest surprised him.

"Yes, I think there is a need, Pike," he said, and Pike nodded.

"I don't understand," Sally said. "Why kill Father O'Neil? Who did it?"

"It's Iron Shield's way of tellin' us that he hasn't forgotten us," McConnell said.

"Iron Shield?" she said, surprised. "But . . . but I thought that Brave Wolf said Father O'Neil would be safe?"

"Iron Shield has a mind of his own, Sally," Pike said. "It doesn't matter to him what Brave Wolf *or* Crying Bear might have said."

"But . . . but . . ."

"Never mind, Sally," Pike said. "Don't try to understand it."

Pike, McConnell, and Father Santini all walked to where Father Smets was kneeling by the body of Father O'Neil.

"Excuse me, Father," Pike said, and carefully wrapped the body in the blanket again. "But it's time to bury him now."

Later, Father Smets prayed again over the grave of Father O'Neil, while the others stood by quietly. Pike's initial anger had faded, but he did not regret making Father Smets view the body. The older man *had* to understand that up here in the mountains things were completely different from the world he had come from. Pike felt that Father O'Neil's death was avoidable. All they had had to do was take him with them when they left. They had *all* avoided death, and then they had turned around and left the terrified man to his own.

It was such a waste.

But he was angry at himself too, because he could have prevented this from happening. If he had insisted that Father O'Neil accompany the rest of them when they left the Blackfoot camp, the man would still be alive. He had known what would happen if they left him there, and yet he didn't argue the point.

And how about putting some blame on Father O'Neil himself? As frightened as the man had been, he had agreed to stay behind. He could have saved himself by insisting that he wouldn't stay. Had he been courageous, or simply stupid?

McConnell fell in next to his friend. "It's not your fault," he said.

"I know."

"You did what you could."

"I'm not blaming myself."

"Sure you are."

Pike hesitated. "Okay, maybe I am, a little, but it's mostly their fault."

"Iron Shield and his people?"

Pike shook his head.

"Iron Shield and Father Smets."

Now it was McConnell's turn to hesitate. "I guess I can't really argue with that," he said momentarily.

"But maybe," Pike said, "just maybe, if I had insisted . . ."

Thirty-One

Their progress was solemn after that. The death of Father O'Neil had its effect on each of them. Father Santini still appeared to be in shock. Sally and Glory seemed to take turns breaking out into tears and comforting one another. Pike and McConnell remained silent. Pike noticed that Father Smets seemed to have withdrawn into himself. The look on his face was still rather serene, but Pike hoped that there was some turmoil going on inside the man. He would have liked it better if the older man had shown some grief. He didn't need him to question his faith, just show some emotion.

They rode the remainder of the day without incident, and then camped. Pike still had the distinct feeling that they were being watched, but he didn't realize just how *many* eyes were on them.

Iron Shield and his followers trailed along behind Pike and the others. The Blackfoot warrior wanted the whites to think a long time about what had happened to their friend. Also, one of his scouts had spotted a Flathead party, and Iron Shield wanted to wait and see just where they were going. Maybe he'd let the white and the Flatheads battle, and then come in and pick up the pieces.

"Why don't we go down and talk to them?" Father Gentry asked Red Hawk. From this distance all Father Gentry could tell was that the people were white. He could not identify them further, although one of the priests did have white hair.

"No," Red Hawk said. "We wait."

"Why?"

"Blackfeet close by."

"Blackfeet?" Father Gentry said. "What are they doing around here?"

"Don't know," Red Hawk said. "But we wait and see." Red Hawk had learned his English from Father Gentry, and he was very proud of it.

"Red Hawk," the priest said, "why don't you let me go down and talk to them? You could stay here and watch for the Blackfeet."

"Too dangerous," Red Hawk said.

"For who?" Father Gentry asked. "Not for me. They won't do anything to hurt me, but if they see you, something might happen. Someone might misunderstand what's happening."

Red Hawk thought it over and then shook his head. "Too dangerous."

"No, it's not," Father Gentry said. "Come on, Red Hawk. Dark Horse and Strong Hand must be wondering what happened to us."

Finally, Red Hawk agreed.

"But we wait until they make camp."

"All right, Red Hawk," the priest said, "you're in charge."

Red Hawk nodded with satisfaction, and Father Gentry hid a smile.

They were camped only a short while and preparing their meal when Pike stood up, cocking his head to one side.

"I hear it, too," McConnell said.

"Hear what?" Sally asked.

"A horse," McConnell said. "One rider approaching."

"I don't hear—" Father Smets started, but Pike silenced him with a quick, "Shh!"

They waited, all of them listening, and finally the others heard what Pike and McConnell had heard long before, the sound of an approaching horse.

McConnell stood up next to Pike, and although neither man was holding his rifle, the guns were within easy reach, if needed.

Finally, the riding form came into the camp, into the light thrown by the campfire. It was a white man, a priest, riding an Indian pony, and he was alone.

"Father Gentry?" Father Smets said in disbelief.

Father Gentry, younger than Father Smets but older than Father Santini, smiled and slid down from the pony.

"Father Smets," he said.

Father Smets rushed to the man and they embraced heartily.

"I can't believe it's you," Father Smets said, holding the younger man at arm's length.

"You came all this way," Father Gentry said, "you must have thought you'd find me."

"Hoped, my boy," Father Smets said. "I hoped to find you, but I don't know if I ever really expected to."

Father Smets walked Father Gentry to the fire and introduced him to everyone. When he was told Pike's name he said, "Ah, He Whose Head Touches the Sky. I've heard much about you."

"Cup of coffee, Father?" McConnell asked. "I'll bet it's been a long time between cups."

"Yes, it has."

McConnell poured one and gave it to the man, who sipped it and then rolled his eyes.

"Oh my, that's good."

"Sit down, Father," Pike said. "I imagine you and Father Smets have a lot to talk about. I hope you don't mind if we listen in."

"I don't mind," Father Gentry said.

"Where are the others, Father?" Father Smets asked. "Are they safe? Where have you been all these years? What have you been doing?"

"Father, I don't think we should talk about that now," Father Gentry said. "There are other, more pressing matters at the moment."

"Did you come with a party, Father?" Pike asked.

"Yes," Father Gentry said. "They're out there right now, but there are also some Blackfeet in the area."

"We know," Pike said, "they're after us."

"After you?" Father Gentry repeated. "Why?"

"That's also something we can talk about later," Pike said. "Can you take us back to your camp?"

"That's what the chief, Strong Hand, sent us out here to do," the priest said, "but we'll have to wait until morning."

"That's fine," Pike said. "With Blackfoot *and* Flathead parties out there, I don't think anyone is going to make any moves tonight. We'll set a watch, just the same."

"I think that's wise," Father Gentry said. He looked

at McConnell and asked, "Could I have some more of that coffee?"

"Sure, Father," McConnell said. "And something to eat. Supper's almost ready."

They all ate around the fire while Father Smets told Father Gentry everything that had happened to them. When he told Gentry about Sister Mary, the other man nodded his head with sad understanding, and then again when he heard about Father O'Neil.

"I know how you feel, Father," he said. "Some of my party were also killed."

"Oh, no," Father Smets said. "Father Callahan?"

"Yes," Gentry said, "and Brother David."

"Oh, no," Father Smets said again. "What about Sister Margaret and Sister Florinda?"

"They are . . . still alive," Father Gentry said, but Pike had the distinct impression there was something that he *wasn't* saying.

"Thank God for that," Father Smets said. "Tell me, Father, about the Flathead Indians. Have they treated you well? What have you learned? Have you made much progress with them?"

Pike leaned over to McConnell and said, "I'll take the first watch, starting now."

McConnell nodded and Pike picked up his rifle and left the campfire. He wasn't really interested in the conversation between the two priests. He had been sitting only a few minutes when Sally joined him.

"Do you mind some company?"

"No," he said, "sit down."

He moved over and she sat next to him, her hips pressed firmly to his.

"I guess we'll be in the Flathead camp tomorrow," she said.

"Looks like it," he said. "With Father Gentry already

there, you'll probably be welcome."

"That means you and Skins will be moving on, doesn't it?"

"I suppose it does, yes."

"Think you'll be back this way any time in the future?" she asked.

He looked at her. "I don't know about that, Sally. All I can say is that it's not impossible."

She nodded. "I understand. You have your life, and we . . . we have ours."

"Do you, Sally?" he asked.

"What do you mean?"

"Do you have your own life?" he said again. "Is this what you really want to do with your life?"

She hesitated before answering, as if gathering her thoughts.

"Three years ago I didn't know what I wanted to do with my life, Pike," she said. "I just knew that it had to change."

"Well, it did that."

"Yes, it did," she said, "drastically. I went from being a whore to serving God."

"You can serve God, Sally, without giving up your life, can't you?"

"According to Father Smets, serving God is a lifetime thing, something that requires all your time."

"I suppose for him it is," Pike said, "but not for you, Sally. You're still young. You shouldn't be stuck up here, living with the Flathead Indians. Where's the future in that for you? Or for Glory? She's even younger, she should be deciding what she wants to do with the rest of her life. I don't want to frighten you—or maybe I do—but if you stay up here, the rest of your life may not be very long."

"I realize that."

"Father Smets, Father Santini, and Father Gentry can do what they want here with the Indians, without your help. There are those other two sisters, right? What were their names?"

"Sister Margaret and Sister Florinda."

"That makes five missionaries up here," he said, "If you ask me, that's more than enough."

She didn't answer, but her entire manner had become hesitant.

"Look," he said, "I'm not trying to talk you out of doing something you really want to do, but make sure you really want to do it. Talk to Glory and make up your minds. If you want, Skins and I will take you with us when we leave. You can go back East, or you can make a life in a settlement up here. Anything is better than . . . than this."

She leaned against him, so that the entire right side of her body pressed against the left side of his, but this was only for a moment, and then she leaned away and stood up.

"I'll think it over, Pike," she said.

"And talk to Glory."

"Yes," she said, "I'll talk to Glory. Good night. I'll see you in the morning."

Pike watched her walk away and hoped that she would seriously consider everything he had said. He would hate to see Sally and Glory end up as Flathead squaws—or worse.

Father Smets and Father Gentry sat at the fire and talked for hours, until Pike walked over to them.

"Excuse me, gents, but you'd better get some sleep if you want to get an early start in the morning."

"Pike is right," Father Smets said. "We have a lot of

time ahead of us for talking. We had better turn in."

"All right," Father Gentry said.

"I'll get you a blanket," Father Smets said to Father Gentry, leaving him at the fire with Pike.

"Can we make the Flathead camp tomorrow, Father?" Pike asked.

"Yes," Gentry said, "we'll be there by noon. In the morning I'll just call to Red Hawk and the others and they'll come down to join us and escort us back."

"Fine."

"Mr. Pike?" Father Gentry called as Pike turned to return to his post.

"Yes?"

"Excuse me for asking, but is there something about me you don't like?"

Pike turned to face the man. "Well, now that you ask, Father, there is."

"And what is that?"

"You're not being honest with Father Smets."

"Oh? In what way am I being dishonest?"

"You're not telling him everything," Pike said. "You're holding something back, Father, and I hope it's worth it to you when he finds out what it is."

"Mr. Pike, I—"

Pike held up his hand and said, "Whatever it is, I don't want to know. It's really none of my business, and I'll find out anyway at the same time he does. Just think about what I said."

Pike turned without giving the man a chance to reply and walked off.

Thirty-Two

McConnell woke Pike early the next morning by calling out to him. Pike came immediately awake.

"What is it?" he asked, bolting out of his blanket with his rifle in his hand.

"A horse approaching," McConnell said. "Sounds like it's unshod."

"What's that mean?" Sally asked. She had also come awake when she heard Pike's name called.

"An Indian pony," Pike said.

"Aren't we expecting Father Gentry's Indians?" she asked.

"Not until he signals them," Pike said.

The others were also awakening at the sound of a disturbance.

"Quiet," Pike told them all. "We'll know soon enough what's in store."

They waited while the horse came closer, and when it moved into sight and entered the camp McConnell headed it off and stopped it. The rider on its back was dead, tied to the animal.

"Flathead," he called out to Pike.

"Oh, no," Father Gentry said.

Pike reached McConnell first, and then Father

Gentry. Pike took hold of the dead Indian's hair and pulled the head up so they could see his face.

"Do you know him, Father Gentry?"

"Yes," Father Gentry said, closing his eyes. "It's my friend, Red Hawk." He opened his eyes and said to Pike, "Please release his hair."

Pike set the Indian's head back down and released his hold.

"Father Gentry, I think you'd better give your signal. If there are any of your Flathead Indians out there, we're going to need them."

"I don't—you think they're *all* dead?" Father Gentry asked.

"I guess we're about to find that out, aren't we?" Pike said.

While Father Gentry waved his signal McConnell moved around the other side of the pony to examine the three arrows that were sticking out of Red Hawk's back.

"Blackfoot arrows, Pike," McConnell said. "It looks like Iron Shield has made his move."

McConnell walked the horse to the other side of the camp and released it. They waited about fifteen minutes before someone spoke.

"I guess that answers our question," Pike said, "Iron Shield and his braves must have killed the Flathead braves. How many were there, Father?"

"Counting Red Hawk, there were six," Father Gentry said. "They're all dead?"

"It looks that way, Father," Pike said. "We're on our own. Can you find your way back to the Flathead camp?"

"I—I believe so."

"Will we get there in time?" Sally asked. "I mean, before Iron Shield comes for us?"

"Probably not," Pike said, "but we can't just stay

here, so we might as well get started."

They broke camp quickly, but not frantically. Pike warned them all not to seem panicky, because he could see the terror in the eyes of Glory and Father Santini. Pike explained that if they seemed frightened or panicky, Iron Shield would probably just swoop down on them and wipe them out.

"We want him to keep playing with us," he explained.

"Why?" Sally asked.

"As long as he's playing with us," McConnell said, "we're still alive."

Sally stared at him and then shuddered.

Iron Shield was very pleased with himself. It was a stroke of genius to kill the Flathead braves—and it had been so easy—and then send one of them to Pike as a message. The Blackfoot brave had to admire Pike's reaction, though. While the others in his party undoubtedly felt fear, Pike kept control of them, and of himself.

He was a worthy adversary, and it would be a great pleasure to kill him.

Progress was slow. It became obvious that Father Gentry did not know the way back to the camp, but that he was trying to feel his way. They had to double back more than once when Father Gentry realized he was on the wrong track.

At one point Pike called their progress to a halt so he could speak to Father Gentry.

"Father," Pike said, "I know this is difficult."

"Do you?" Gentry asked. "As a man of God I should not fear death, and yet I do."

"Maybe it's not death you fear," Pike said, "but dying."

"What's the difference?"

"There are better ways to die than at the hands of the Blackfoot Indians, Father."

After a moment Gentry said, "Yes, I suppose you're right. It's the dying."

"The trick to retracing your steps," Pike said, "is to look for landmarks. An outcropping of rock, an odd-shaped tree or bush, something like that."

Father Gentry nodded and then gave Pike a grateful look.

"I'm having trouble concentrating," he said, "I'm . . . a little nervous."

"We're all more than a little nervous, Father," Pike said. "Just do the best you can."

"You're very kind, Mr. Pike," Father Gentry said, "but I know that our lives depend on my finding the way back."

"Yes," Pike said, "they do, but take comfort in this. Iron Shield will probably never let us reach your camp. As soon as he sees we're going in the right direction, that's when he'll make his move."

"Then . . . what's the point?"

"The point, Father Gentry, is to keep trying."

"Is everything all right?" McConnell asked, riding up next to them.

Father Gentry held Pike's eyes for a moment longer, then looked at McConnell. "Yes, yes, everything is fine."

"We'd better keep moving, Father," McConnell said.

"Yes," Father Gentry said, looking around them, "this way."

McConnell looked at Pike. "At least we're not going in circles . . . yet," he said.

232

* * *

Sometime later Father Gentry said, "There."

"What?" Pike asked.

"I recognize that rock formation. I remember thinking that it looked like a cluster of rock candy."

"Very good," Pike said. "It means we're headed in the right direction."

Which also meant that Iron Shield was bound to make his move very soon.

Pike wished that someone else had guns besides him and McConnell. Sally still had the Kentucky pistol he had given her long ago, but he doubted that she would use it.

Come on, Iron Shield, he thought, get it over with.

"Yes, yes," Father Gentry said sometime later, "this is the right way all right." He looked at Pike with a gleam of satisfaction in his eyes. "This is the way."

Pike was about to congratulate the priest when he heard a scream. He turned and saw an arrow imbedded in Father Santini's thigh. The man screamed and kept screaming . . .

Thirty-Three

Pike leaped from his horse. His concern was for Sally. He wanted to get her off her horse and to cover. The others would have to fend for themselves.

Sally had frozen in place, staring at Father Santini. The man was still screaming when a second arrow pierced his chest. He looked down at it with eyes that were mostly whites and began screaming anew, even louder than before.

Pike grabbed Sally by the arm and pulled her down from her horse.

"Come on," he said. "We've got to get to cover."

She was in a panic and was fighting him without realizing what she was doing. An arrow struck her horse and the animal rolled its eyes, screamed, and started to fall toward them. Pike had to pull her by the arm again, so that neither of them would be pinned beneath it. He then lifted her in his arms and ran for cover with her.

Once they were behind some rocks he set her down too hard. She'd end up with a bruised ass—if they lived through this, which was doubtful.

Pike looked around for the others. McConnell had apparently done the same thing for Glory that he had done for Sally, and the two of them had taken cover also.

Satisfied that McConnell was all right, he looked around for Father Smets and Father Gentry. It was only then that he realized that Father Santini had stopped screaming. He saw that the man had fallen from his horse and was lying on the ground. He also saw that Father Smets was kneeling next to him.

"Father Smets!" he called. "Find some cover!"

The man gave no indication that he had heard. Pike looked again for McConnell, who was farther from Father Smets than he was. He looked around for Father Gentry and saw that the man had also taken cover. He, too, was farther from Father Smets than Pike.

He turned and looked at Sally, who was sobbing uncontrollably.

"Sally," he said, then grabbed her arm and shook her roughly. "Sally! Look at me! Come on!"

Finally, she turned her eyes on him.

"Stay right here. Don't move. Understand? Don't move from here."

He didn't know if she understood or not, but he couldn't wait any longer. He had to get to Father Smets before the priest was killed.

Pike looked over at McConnell and mimed what he intended to do. McConnell replied in kind that he would cover him.

Abruptly, Pike stood and moved out from behind his cover. He ran to Father Smets and grabbed the man under the arms. He found him remarkably light.

"Please," Father Smets said, "I must give him last rites."

But the priest did not resist while Pike dragged him to safety. As he pulled him behind the rocks several arrows fell around them, but none came close.

Iron Shield was still playing games.

Nothing happened for half an hour.

"What are they waiting for?" Father Smets asked.

"Iron Shield wants us to think about dying," Pike said, "about *how* we're going to die."

Pike was aware that Sally, who was next to him, had taken control of herself and had stopped crying. He reached out and put his hand on her shoulder.

"Are you all right?"

She looked at him. "I can still hear him screaming."

"I know," Pike said, "I know."

"There must be something we can do," Father Smets said. "Perhaps I can talk to Iron Shield."

"Remember our agreement, Father," Pike said. "You'll do what I tell you to do."

"Yes, but . . . all this killing," Father Smets said, shaking his head. Pike waited for the man to argue further, but to his surprise he did not. For some reason the death of Father Santini seemed to have hit him harder than the death of Father O'Neil. Or maybe it was the combination of the two deaths that was affecting him. Whatever it was, he seemed to withdraw into a subdued silence that Pike was grateful for.

"We have to do something," Sally said mournfully. "We can't just . . . die."

"Well," Pike said, "there is one thing we can try."

"What?" she asked.

"I don't know if it will work, but . . ." Pike got to his feet and stuck his head out from cover.

"Iron Shield!" he called. "Iron Shield, can you hear me?"

There was a moment of silence and then Iron Shield's voice rang out.

237

"I hear you!"

"Let the others go, Iron Shield," Pike said. "It's me you want."

"No!" Sally got to her knees and grabbed Pike's arm. "You can't do that! Father, he can't do that!"

Pike shook off her hand and yelled, "What do you say, Iron Shield?"

"I say no, white man," Iron Shield called back. "You will all die, and you will go last."

Pike looked down at Sally. "See? He's not going for it."

"I'm glad he didn't accept," she said. "I couldn't go on living knowing you gave up your life."

Pike only half heard her. He was thinking of something else to try.

"Let's see how he reacts to this," he said, half to himself.

"What?" Sally said.

"Iron Shield!" Pike yelled. "Come out and fight me like a warrior! Or are you afraid?"

"No! You can't do that either!" Sally said desperately.

"If I can kill him," Pike said, "the others might leave us alone."

"What do you say to that, Iron Shield?" he yelled. "Or are you a cowardly dog who does his fighting only from hiding?"

There was a long, deadly silence before Iron Shield responded.

"You will have your battle, white man," he called out, "but only *after* all of your friends are dead. I will let you fight, but only for your own life. Only after you have watched the others die."

"Iron Shield is an old woman," Pike called out, but he knew it was no use.

When Iron Shield did not respond Pike looked at

Sally and said, "This is not good. He's being smart about this. He's not allowing me to goad him."

"Then we're going to die."

"Well, if we are," Pike said, "we'll take as many of them with us as possible. Where is that Kentucky pistol I gave you?"

She gave him a sad look and said, "I'm sorry. It's on my horse."

Pike looked out at Sally's horse, which was lying dead on the ground.

"In that case Skins and I are just going to have to do the best we can," he said. Luckily, when he jumped from his horse his possibles bag and powder horn had been hanging on his shoulders. He removed them and placed them on the ground. Once they charged, he didn't know how many times he'd be able to reload and fire before they were on top of them. He knew one thing, though. Iron Shield would not spare Sally and Glory. This time he would kill them all. Pike knew he had to spare Sally that by saving *his* last shot for her.

Thirty-Four

When nothing happened for two hours Pike decided to try to get to Sally's fallen horse. They could use the pistol and possibles that were there, not to mention the water. When he stepped out from behind the rocks he was using for cover, an arrow appeared in the ground so quickly it seemed to have blossomed there.

"I guess they're still out there," Pike said, ducking back behind the rocks.

"Can't we run away?" Sally asked. "Can't we run this way?" She pointed behind them.

"Sally," Pike said, "there's nowhere to go, not on foot."

"Maybe we can find our horses."

"Iron Shield wouldn't give us time to do that," Pike said.

"Well, we've got to do something."

"We are."

"What?"

"Right now we're waiting."

"Well, that doesn't seem to be very productive," she complained. She looked at Pike then and said, "I'm sorry, I'm just—"

"I know," Pike said, "I know. You're right, we've got

to do something other than wait. I *might* be able to slip away and find one horse. You and Glory could share it. We could try to hold them off until you got away."

"No, I won't leave without you," she said, then looked at Father Smets and said, "without the rest of you."

But Pike was beginning to warm to the idea.

"Sally, I believe that if you and Glory made a run for it, Iron Shield wouldn't follow you. He'd stay here because, in the end, it's me he really wants."

"You could get killed trying to find a horse."

Pike rubbed his jaw and said, "Skins could do it. I just have to get over to him and let him know what we're planning."

"How are you going to do that?"

"I'll run," Pike said, and got up very quickly before he could change his mind and did just that. He ran toward McConnell while arrows fell behind him. He virtually slid the last few feet, before some smart Indian could cause him to run into an arrow.

"What the hell are you doin' here?" McConnell asked.

"Just being neighborly," Pike said, sitting down next to McConnell. He looked past his friend at Glory, who was staring at nothing.

"How long has she been like that?" Pike asked.

"Since Father Santini died," McConnell said. "I try talking to her, but I don't think she can hear me."

"She might be better off," Pike said. "Listen, I've got an idea."

He explained to McConnell what he thought they could do with one horse.

"So all one of us has to do is go out there and find a horse," McConnell said.

"Right," Pike said. "You go."

"I like being given a choice."

"We don't have a choice," Pike said. "If I go . . ." and he trailed off, as something occurred to him.

"Yeah?" McConnell said, waiting for his friend to finish.

"If I go," Pike continued slowly, "they'll probably follow me."

"And that's why you want *me* to go?"

"No, no," Pike said, "you don't understand. I was going to stay so that Iron Shield would stay, figuring that he wants me more than anyone else."

"That makes sense," McConnell said in agreement. "I'll go."

"No," Pike said, "it's better if I go."

"Now you're confusing me."

"No, it's simple," Pike said. "I make it look like I'm running away. Iron Shield will come after me, and the rest of you can escape. You may even find some of the horses nearby."

"What if he leaves most of his braves to watch us?" McConnell asked.

"I don't think he will," Pike said. "I think he'll want me so badly that he'll come after me himself, and bring most of his braves with him. I think it's a chance we have to take."

"Well," McConnell said, "at least it's a chance. When do you want to go?"

"No time like now," Pike said. "Here." He handed McConnell his rifle. His friend took it, giving him an odd look. "You'll need it more than I will if some braves come after you," Pike explained.

"But you won't be armed."

"Hell, man," Pike said, "what good is one rifle going to do me if ten braves come after me? You, on the other hand, might have enough firepower to help you and the others get away."

"Pike," McConnell said, "your end of this sounds

243

like a suicide mission."

"Don't kid yourself, Skins," Pike said, "you'll be in as much danger as I will."

McConnell didn't necessarily agree, but when he took into consideration that Pike would only have to fend for himself, while McConnell had the others in his charge, he figured the danger evened out.

"What will you tell Sally and the others?" McConnell asked.

"Nothing," Pike said. "I'll just move out from here."

"Sally's gonna think you're runnin'."

Pike smiled. "No she won't."

Pike got up onto his haunches and risked a peek to see if he could spot any Indians.

"Where do you figure they are?" he asked McConnell.

"I haven't been able to see any of them, but my guess would be high ground."

"Yeah, that'd be my guess too."

Pike looked around, taking time to pick out his direction. He actually *wanted* Iron Shield to see him running away, but he didn't want to make it too obvious what he was doing. It was doubtful that the Blackfoot brave would think Pike was trying to get away. It was more likely he'd think Pike was trying for a horse, or even trying to circle around to the other side of the braves. Of course, that was out, because Pike didn't know where they were.

"I'll go this way," Pike said, pointing back down the way they had come. "I think I saw a couple of horses run off in that direction."

"All right."

"If you see an Indian pop his head up," Pike said, "do me a favor and shoot it off."

"I'll do it."

Pike slapped McConnell on the shoulder. "Good luck."

"You, too."

Pike moved to the very edge of their cover, and then started running.

When Iron Shield saw Pike run from cover to cover he instructed his braves *not* to kill him. They simply fired some arrows down at him to let him know that they were still there. Now, however, Pike was not running back the way he had come, but seemed to be running *away*.

"He is running away," one of his braves said.

"No," Iron Shield said thoughtfully, "not away. He is running *to* something."

"To what?" the brave asked.

"A horse," Iron Shield said.

"He *is* running away," the brave said.

"No," Iron Shield said, getting to his feet, "he wants a horse for the women. Stay here with Little Horse and Tall Bear. I will take the others and catch Pike."

Iron Shield pointed to the two braves that were to stay behind, then waved his arm imperiously. The other nine braves fell in behind him.

Pike ran, but he was careful not to run too hard. After all, he didn't *really* want to get away from the Blackfeet. Not yet, anyway. Holding back wasn't hard, either, because running aggravated his healing wound.

He soon became aware that he was being pursued. He heard horses behind him, and that was when he spotted McConnell's horse up ahead of him. If he truly wanted nothing but to get away, this would have been his opportunity. He might have been able to mount that horse and outrun the Blackfoot braves. Some of them would probably chase him, but some of the others would probably go back for McConnell and the others. Of course, McConnell might have already gotten them away—without a shot fired?—but he couldn't take that chance.

As he approached the horse he lost his balance and fell heavily to the ground. Before he knew it he was surrounded by Iron Shield and nine braves on horseback. It was that simple, the difference between getting away and getting caught.

Thirty-Five

"Let's go," McConnell said to Glory, but she didn't move. He stood up, waved his arms, and shouted to the others, "Go, go, go!"

He leaned over Glory and slapped her across the face. Suddenly, her eyes focused on him, and began to fill with tears.

"There's no time to cry," he said, pulling her to her feet. "Come on!"

He ran, pulling her with him. When he saw Father Smets, Father Gentry, and Sally they were confused, unsure of which way to run.

"Jesus," he said. He couldn't point because he was holding Glory with one hand, and trying to hold onto both his rifle and Pike's with the other.

As he reached them he thrust the rifles at Father Gentry and said, "Take one."

"I can't!" the priest said, shocked.

"I just want you to carry it," McConnell snapped. "Take it, damn it!"

Father Gentry took the rifle and held it awkwardly.

"Sally, take Glory's hand."

Sally obeyed, taking the other girl's hand from him.

"Now let's move, that way," he said, pointing ahead

of them. "Go!"

"Where's Pike?" Sally asked.

"Never mind," he said, shoving her. "Go!"

They started running, McConnell staying at the others' heels even though he could have passed them easily. He risked a look behind and saw that three braves had come down from high ground and were chasing them.

"Father Gentry!"

Gentry heard him, turned, and saw the Indians.

"Give me the rifle and keep running."

"What about you?"

McConnell took the second rifle and said, "Keep them running. You might find some horses. If you do, get on them and ride, and don't stop until you get to the Flathead camp. Understand?"

McConnell didn't wait for an answer. He turned, fell to one knee, set one rifle down on the ground, and lifted the other to his shoulder. His first shot struck a brave in the chest, knocking him down. McConnell quickly set down the empty rifle and picked up the loaded one. Coolly, he lined up his shot and pulled the trigger. Another brave fell to the ground.

The third brave kept running, and McConnell stood up and reversed the rifle, holding it by the barrel, and waited . . .

At the sound of the first shot, Iron Shield lifted his head, looking away from Pike. Then he looked down, as if trying to find something, and Pike knew he was looking for a rifle.

"Where is your weapon?" the Indian asked.

The sound of the second shot answered his question for him. Pike could see the anger in the man's eyes as he realized he had been duped. Even if he had sent three or four braves after McConnell, Pike knew Skins well enough to feel that he had a good chance of getting the missionaries away safely.

And that had been the whole idea.

Pike was still on his back. Iron Shield turned and said something Pike didn't catch, waving his arm. Three braves turned their ponies and ran back toward the shooting. Pike felt he had to do something. Heaving with all his weight, he leaped off the ground and ran at the mounted Indian. He caught the man around the waist and pulled him from his horse in one mighty motion. The three braves who were riding away stopped and turned to see what was happening. Pike was convinced he was a dead man, but he hoped he was giving McConnell and the others precious moments to escape.

Iron Shield was stunned at first, but soon regained his stance and fought hard. The two men rolled around on the ground for a few moments, Pike just holding on, trying to keep Iron Shield from getting to his feet or shouting orders. He wasn't even throwing any punches, he was simply holding on, wanting to give the others time. It was only then that he realized he still had his knife.

While the other braves watched their leader grapple with the white man, Pike used his strength and weight to pin Iron Shield to the ground, then pulled out his knife and thrust it into the Blackfoot warrior's belly. Iron Shield's eyes went wide, filled with anger and surprise, then suddenly went blank.

Pike stood up, staring down at the dead warrior, then looked up at the nine Blackfoot braves who had once again surrounded him. They stared at him, then at their fallen leader, then back at him.

Pike raised his knife and waited.

Suddenly, the sound of horses filled the air as about

twenty Flathead Indians appeared from the direction of the shooting.

Almost immediately they heard horses from the other direction. They turned and saw Brave Wolf come into view, leading about ten Blackfoot warriors.

The tableau was set. In the center was Pike and the Blackfoot braves who had followed Iron Shield. On one side Brave Wolf and ten braves, on the other side twenty Flathead braves.

From behind the Flathead came McConnell and the missionaries.

"Oh my God," Sally said when she saw the situation Pike was in. "What can we do?"

"Wait," McConnell said, "just wait. This has to resolve itself."

So they waited.

Pike didn't move. He felt the same way McConnell did, that he was just going to have to wait and see what happened.

The Blackfoot and the Flathead braves eyed one another, and then Brave Wolf dismounted and walked toward Pike. When he reached him he looked down at Iron Shield's body.

"He was always out of control," Brave Wolf said. "He could have been a great warrior."

Pike remained silent.

Brave Wolf looked up at the nine warriors who had followed Iron Shield and made an abrupt motion with his arm. Slowly, they rode over to where the other Blackfoot braves were gathered.

"You will have no further trouble with the Blackfeet," Brave Wolf said to Pike.

"Thank you, Brave Wolf."

Brave Wolf walked back to his braves, mounted his

pony, gestured for the others to follow him, and then rode off.

Pike turned and saw Sally running toward him, with McConnell walking behind her. Father Gentry was standing in front of the Flathead braves, talking to them. Father Smets was off to one side with an arm around Glory.

Epilogue

When they rode into the Flathead camp they found out that Red Hawk's horse, with him still tied to it, had found its way back to the camp, which had caused Strong Hand to send out twenty braves to find out what had happened.

"I guess they saved our bacon," McConnell said, "but it sure could have gotten a lot worse when Brave Wolf showed up."

"I thought I was dead for sure," Pike said.

Sally was between them as they walked through the Flathead camp. Ahead of them, Father Smets walked with Father Gentry. Glory was walking to Father Smets' left. They were waiting for the appearance of Strong Hand.

Suddenly, Father Smets stopped walking, and they stopped behind him.

"What's wrong?" Sally asked.

Father Smets pointed and they looked at a group of women who were sitting together. They were working, mending blankets, making moccasins, and Pike noticed that there were two white women among them, one of whom had bared her breasts to nurse an infant.

Father Smets was still pointing, and his hand was shaking.

"That—that is Sister Florinda!" he said, his voice unsteady.

"The woman with the baby?" Sally asked.

"And that," Father Smets went on, pointing to the other white woman, "is Sister Margaret."

The woman he identified as Sister Florinda looked to be about twenty-five years old. Her hair was long, her breasts swollen with milk. The other white woman looked to be in her forties, but apparently *some* brave had decided to take her as his squaw.

Father Smets was shocked and shaken to see that two women he had known as Catholic nuns had been turned into Flathead squaws.

"What happened?" he demanded, directing an accusatory look at Father Gentry.

"No one forced them, Father," Father Gentry said. "We were here a long time, and they were lonely. A young brave expressed an interest in Sister Florinda, and she reciprocated. She consented to become his wife. The baby was born only last month."

"And what did you say to her?" Father Smets asked.

"She came to me, Father," Father Gentry said, "and I gave her my blessing."

"You *what?*"

"Sister Margaret was also asked by one of the older braves to be his squaw, and she agreed. I also gave her my blessing."

"Father Gentry," Father Smets said, "what were you thinking? They are servants of God. How could you allow them to forsake their vows?"

"Father," Father Gentry said, putting his arm around the older man's shoulder, "let me try to explain . . ." and the two men walked off together. Glory didn't seem to know where to go, so she moved over next to McConnell.

"As I understand it," McConnell said to Pike, "Strong Hand wanted Father Gentry to stay, but the medicine man, Dark Horse, wanted him killed. I guess the two of them will disagree over what to do about Father Smets and these girls."

Pike looked at Sally and said, "Let's go for a walk."

They walked away from McConnell and Glory.

"Do you see what happened?" Pike asked.

"What do you mean?"

"Sister Florinda and Sister Margaret are now Flathead squaws, Sally. Do you want that to happen to you?"

"Nobody forced them, Pike."

"The loneliness forced them into it, Sally."

"I have to stay, Pike," Sally said. "This trip has been very hard on Father Smets, and now to find this out . . . he needs me."

"And Glory?"

"Glory feels the same way."

"Well . . ." Pike said, "I guess all that remains is to see if Strong Hand will let you stay."

McConnell joined them at that moment and said, "Strong Hand has appeared."

"It looks like we're going to find that out now," Pike said.

Pike and McConnell rode out of the Flathead camp the next day. Just outside of the camp Pike turned and looked back.

"They made their decisions, Pike," McConnell said. "*All* of them. Strong Hand said they could stay, and they all decided to."

"I know that," Pike said.

"They know Dark Horse doesn't want them there,

but they're depending on Strong Hand to keep Dark Horse at bay. It sounds to me a lot like what we went through in the Blackfoot camp. Still, we got them here and the decision to stay is theirs. There's nothing you can do about it."

"I know that, Skins," Pike said, "I just hope they don't regret the decision."

"We could always come back this way in a few months and check," McConnell offered.

"Yeah," Pike said, turning his horse, "we *could*."